Mr. Breeze

a Novel

Morrie Richfield

ISBN: 0615461034
ISBN-13: 9780615461038

The Book is dedicated to my sons Taylor and Jake
Never stop dreaming boys you never know when they might come true

And

To the Grateful Dead
Thanks for the music and the memories

Acknowledgments

I would like to express my thanks to:

Cassie, for doing her best
Joan, for making this readable
My dogs Bear Bear and Baby and my cat Suni for keeping me company at 4:00am for ten months while I wrote this.
My little sis Nancy for putting up with me all these years
And Special Thanks To
M.F. for bringing the light back in my life

I am quite certain that there are many ways in which I could tell you this story. I think the best way is to start at the beginning and just let the story unfold itself. It is the story of how I came to meet the man who would end up changing the world as we know it, the man we would all come to know as Mr. Breeze.

My name is Michael Ryan. I am what you would call a freelance photojournalist. At the age of fifty-two, I had spent more than twenty years chasing one story or another, and I was fairly sure that I had seen pretty much everything. I was soon about to find out just how wrong I was.

In the beginning of the year 2010, the world was as unsettled as it had ever been prior to the start of the Second World War. Every day there were new atrocities making front-page headlines in newspapers all over the world. It was certainly a time when we all needed something to lift our spirits, something to make us feel a little better about ourselves and the world around us.

It was with that in mind that I decided to search through hundreds of newspapers all over the country for stories about the goodness in people. It did not matter whether the story was about a five-year-old raising money selling cookies to help the homeless or the fireman who pulled an elderly woman out of a burning building. My plan was to compile these stories and attempt sell the idea of a special edition to one of the major publications. I had no idea where it would end up taking me.

I hired a staff of researchers and set them to work finding the accounts I was looking for. I anticipated it would take about three weeks to compile enough stories to fulfill the requirements I had set. I must admit I was quite surprised when in only three days, my researchers seemed to think they had found something very unusual. My past experiences had hardened me to the point that my first thoughts were always those of a skeptic. When I arrived at the office of my research service company, I hardly expected to find anything of much interest. I would soon find out how incorrect my assumptions were.

My researchers had found over seventy articles which all appeared to involve the same man. In more than twenty different states, this man seemed to be traveling around the country doing your normal good deeds. In other cases, he was performing the seemingly impossible. According to the documents we read, he had helped people rebuild their homes after a flood and healed a child who had been hit by a car. In each article there was a description of this man, but not one of the stories contained a picture of this so-called miracle worker. My researchers were right: even though this was certainly not what I had in mind when I started this project, it was the type of challenge I could not resist and I had to find out more. I took the copies of the stories with me and decided to delve a little deeper into this mystery man.

The first thing I needed to do was to contact the journalists who had written the articles to see if I could get a better feel for who this man was. I anticipated that most of what was written had to be nothing more than embellished eyewitness accounts, but my curiosity had gotten the better of me and I was determined to speak with the author of every story.

In the first week following my researchers' discovery of the stories, I managed to contact a dozen authors. After each conversation, I became ever more intrigued by this mystery man. I found that the authors were quite eager to share their knowledge about him with me. I asked why none of their stories contained his name, and they told me he never gave his name. The last thing I asked each of them was why there was no picture of the man in their articles, and they all gave me the same answer. "Funny you should ask," they told me. "We took photographs, but none of them came out." I kept to myself the fact that all the other eleven cameras seemed to have the same problem. I suddenly began to get that feeling I would always get when I was onto something big: This was far more than a simple story about a traveling do-gooder.

It was Friday night and, like every Friday, I met my good friend Al Bishop for dinner and drinks at our favorite local spot. I told Al about everything I had found out so far and his reaction surprised me. Al was a federal prosecutor and he was even more of a skeptic than I was. "You have that look in your eye, Michael," Al said with a smirk on his face. "You think this guy is more than he appears to be, don't you?"

I told him my instincts led me to believe there was much more to him than just some guy doing good deeds. "Something about this guy," I told Al, "something about him just does not add up."

"So what are you going to do, Michael? Track this guy down and see if he's some sort of guardian angel?"

Al's words did not strike a chord that night and, at that moment, I had no idea that I would end up doing just that. When Al and I said goodnight that evening, he seemed almost as interested in knowing about this man as I was. I promised to keep him informed.

I went home, my mind wandering to a point where sleep was impossible. I kept running possibilities through my mind, and as the night wore on, some of them made me question my grip on reality. When sleep finally came, it was much too short and I awoke the next morning even more determined to solve the mystery that I was not completely sure I had not created in my mind just to satisfy my need to solve it.

By ten o'clock that morning, I was on the phone with a talkative television reporter from a local station in Nashville, Tennessee. He asked me to call him Teddy, or at least that's what I thought he had said, as his accent was a bit thick and he talked as fast as an auctioneer. He had been the first at the scene when the young boy was hit by a car, and the story he told me never even made the news. His bosses said it was too crazy to put on the air. Teddy told me by the time he arrived at the accident scene, the boy was already up and walking around. He described how there was blood everywhere. The car that had hit the boy was badly dented in the front and the windshield was smashed. The boy had bounced off the hood of the car, hit the windshield, and was thrown forty feet into the air. I asked him how the boy could possibly be walking around after a serious collision like that. It was then that Teddy confided to me the part of the story his bosses refused to air. He told me according to the boy's mother and more than twenty eyewitnesses, this man came out of nowhere, leaned over the boy, and ran his hand over the boy's almost lifeless body.

Then, only moments later, the boy sat up, smiled at his mother, and picked himself up off the ground. He was perfectly fine. His clothes were torn and bloody, but the boy did not have so much as a scratch on him.

I asked Teddy if he saw this man. "See him! Hell, I talked to him." I asked Teddy if he was able to get his name. "He told me his name was not important. The only important thing was that the boy was unharmed." Even though I felt certain I already knew the answer, I had to ask Teddy if he managed to get this man on film. "That's another strange thing—our cameras were running the whole time. We got the boy, the mother, the neighbors, hell, even the driver of the car on film, but every time the cameras pointed at this fellow, the film was all blurred."

I thanked Teddy for his help and asked him if he could send me a copy of the tape, and a way to get in contact with the boy's family, if possible. Teddy gave me the family's number right then and promised to overnight a copy of the tape. His only request was that if I ever figured out *who* or *what* this guy was, I would let him know. I promised I would.

I hung up the phone and looked down at the note pad on the desk. The name Emily Thomson was written on it. My fingers seemed to dial the number without my thinking about it. The next thing I knew, there was a voice on the other end of the phone saying hello. "Mrs. Thomson, my name is Michael Ryan. I'm a reporter from Washington, D.C. doing a story about the man who helped your son. Do you mind if I ask you a few questions?"

"It's about time!" she exclaimed. "That man saved my son's life."

"What exactly happened that day?" I asked her.

"My son was playing in the front yard with his friends when his ball rolled into the street. Before any of us could grab him, he ran after it and charged right into the path of that car. My Jimmy was just lying there, mister, and I swear he was dead."

"Dead, Mrs. Thomson? Are you sure he was dead?"

There was a silence over the line. I could hear her trying to hold back her emotions, but they had gotten the better of her. She began to speak again, this time trying to hold back her tears. "My boy's neck was broken, and his bones were sticking out of his skin. Mister, I know what dead is."

"This man, where did he come from? Had you ever seen him before?" I asked her.

"No, sir, I never saw him before. He seemed to come out of nowhere. He just walked over to my Jimmy and ran his hand over his body. It was like nothing I had ever seen before. I saw Jimmy's body go back to normal, just like that. His bones were healed and he just opened his eyes and smiled at me."

"Did you get the name of the man who helped your son?" I asked her once again, feeling sure I knew the answer.

"No, sir. Before I had the chance to thank him, he was gone."

I thanked her for taking the time to speak with me. Before she hung up, she made me promise that I would thank the man when I saw him. I don't think she realized I knew even less about him than she did. I put the receiver back on its cradle, leaned back in my chair, and shook my head. I had just heard two people tell me one of the most unbelievable stories I had ever heard, *and* I made two promises I was not sure I could even keep. I was now even more certain that the deeper I got into this, the more unbelievable it was going to become.

I spent the remainder of the day leaving messages and sending e-mail inquiries to the various reporters who had written the articles that were sitting on my desk. There was one article that especially caught my attention. It was written by Ben Harper, an old friend of mine. Years ago, we had worked together at a paper in New England and now he was working as a feature writer in Atlanta. He'd always had a reputation as a man who thoroughly checked his facts before he wrote a story. The article was about a bus full of senior citizens on their way back from a trip when a tire blew out, sending their bus off the road and into the lake that ran along the highway. I dialed Ben's number, and much to my surprise, he answered on the first ring. After the usual catching up, I questioned him about his story.

At first, he was a little curious about my motives. I must admit to bending the truth just a bit, but I didn't want to share what I had learned with another journalist. "Michael, what's your interest in this?" Ben kept pressing. I don't think he totally bought my writing-about-the-good-in-people storyline. But he did finally break down and start talking–and what a story he had to tell. "Okay, Michael, but you have to promise that you're not going to think I'm crazy." Damn, I thought, another promise to keep.

"Sure, Ben, I promise," I told him, thinking once again I was about to hear another incredible story.

"This is the way it happened, Michael, and there were forty eyewitnesses to this whole thing. A bus full of senior citizens is coming back from a day trip and the front tire on their bus blows out. The driver loses control, crashes through the guardrail, and they end up sitting in a lake in eight feet of water, the entire bus beginning to sink. Then this guy, he comes out of nowhere. He reaches his arm out and gestures like he's motioning for someone to come closer. The bus starts moving toward him and does not stop until it's out of the water and back up on the highway."

"Ben, there is nothing about this in the story you wrote," I reluctantly pointed out.

"What do you think, I'm fucking crazy? Who the hell would have believed me? I would have lost every ounce of credibility I have." I could see he was not sure he even believed what had happened. "But wait, you haven't heard the best part yet," he continued.

"There's more?" I asked him.

"Oh yeah, and this is the really creepy part. Okay, the bus is back on the highway. A lot of these people are seriously hurt. Most of them were not in that good a shape to begin with." Ben suddenly stopped talking and there was just silence on the line.

"Ben are you still there?" I must have asked five or six times before I heard him utter another word.

"Michael, are you sure you're not going to think I'm crazy? Shit, I don't want you throwing this up in my face every time we see each other."

"Come on, Ben, you know me better than that."

"Yeah, I know you. That's why I'm asking," he laughed.

"Alright, here goes. The guy gets on the bus and starts walking down the center looking at each of the passengers. Now remember what I told you—these people were really hurt and some of them were unable to walk on their own even before the crash."

"I remember, Ben," I assured him.

"Okay, so here's the kicker—not only were all their injuries suddenly healed, but the people with prior medical problems were healed too."

"What are you saying?"

"I'm saying the deaf were no longer deaf, and if someone needed a walker, well they didn't need one anymore."

"Let me get this straight, Ben. Are you telling me this guy cured these people of whatever medical condition they had?"

"That is *exactly* what I'm telling you. Now you see why I could not write the whole story."

"Yeah, I can see your point. In your situation, I would have done the same thing."

"I'm telling you, Michael, this whole thing freaked me the fuck out."

"Just in case you think I didn't do a little checking, I took a ride over to the center where these people live. I told the doctor I was doing a follow up. The doctor tells me he has never seen anything like this before."

"Meaning?"

"Meaning most of these people had enough different illnesses to fill an entire medical chart, but every one of them was cured of every ailment they had. One of them was so arthritic that he could barely move. Well, guess what? I saw the guy playing ping-pong."

"So why didn't you pursue this?" I asked.

"Pursue what, Michael? The guy just disappeared into thin air. They told me he was there one minute and fucking gone the next. I'd end up looking like a crazy man chasing after a ghost. No thanks, buddy."

"Did anybody give you a description of this guy?" I asked, hoping maybe I'd get a break.

"Yeah, sure, I got a description. He's young, kind of tall, and very nice looking."

"That fits about a quarter of the male population."

"One more thing. He was white and wearing a red baseball cap with a logo of a horse standing on two legs on the front of it. I managed to figure out it was a Ferrari hat. Alright, Michael, I came clean with you, so tell me what's really going on."

I decided to tell Ben everything I knew so far, even about all the articles I had found. "You think it's the same guy in all of those stories?" Ben asked.

"I don't know, but it's unsettling to think there might be more than one of these guys out there. I still have a lot of people to talk to, and I'm hoping that I can get a few more descriptions of this man before I do anything."

"Do? Michael what the hell do you think you can do?"

"I don't know, but something keeps telling me this is the biggest story I've ever come across."

"You always were a stubborn bastard, Michael. You were never one to give up once you smelled a story."

"Thanks, Ben, I'll take that as a compliment regardless of how you meant it."

We both had a good laugh and then Ben became serious again. "Really, what are you thinking here?"

"I don't know, Ben, maybe I'm just thinking out loud, but if it turns out that this is the same guy, I'm going to go look for him."

"Well, if I didn't have a wife and three kids, I'd be going along with you. You keep in touch and let me know what you end up deciding to do."

"I will Ben," I promised. "You take care. Good talking to you."

"You too, buddy," I heard him say before I hung up the phone.

After our conversation, I just sat there. I was sure that this man he described at the scene of the bus accident had to be the same person in all of the stories. Who was this guy and why did he turn up now? Where did he come from? Why has no one ever come across him before? I had way too many questions in my mind and absolutely no answers. I might have been thinking out loud when I mentioned to Ben that I would go looking for this man, but somehow I knew that if I was going to get any of my questions answered, finding him was the only way it was going to happen.

I managed to reach another seven reporters before I called it a day. Each and every one of them described to me the same type of story, and all of them had omitted the unbelievable parts from the published versions—but they were more than happy to share them with me. I did manage to get two more descriptions of this man, and they matched Ben's to a tee. I learned that he was about five-foot-ten, dark-haired, and he looked to be in his mid-to-late thirties. By the time I got into bed that night, I was exhausted, not from anything physical, but because my mind had been spinning around all day. Sleep came quickly and I was excited to see what tomorrow might bring.

The next morning, I found that I had received a number of e-mail replies in response to my inquiries. One stuck out among the others. It was from a reporter in Cleveland who had written a story about a pregnant woman who was in a car accident. At only five months along, she had to give birth prematurely to twins. She was apparently aware of who I was and knew that I was based out of D.C. She told me she was in town and gave me a number where I could reach her. She said she really would like to talk to me. Her name was Monica Brooks.

I called Ms. Brooks and after the usual friendly banter, she asked if she could meet me for lunch. I found this a bit odd since I had not even had the chance to explain why I had contacted her in the first place. But she was quite insistent, so I decided to meet with her and hear what she had to say.

We met in Chevy Chase, Maryland, at a café not far from the hotel where she was staying. Monica looked to be in her late forties. She was very well dressed and well-spoken, and she seemed quite intelligent. "I have to tell you, Michael. You don't mind if I call you Michael, do you?"

"Please do, Monica. Actually, I would prefer it."

"I'm a big fan of yours. You really are a great writer, and you always seem to get the right angle on a story."

I thanked her for the compliment, hoping this meeting was not for the purpose of inflating my ego. Then she suddenly changed gears and was all business. "Let me get to the reason I wanted to meet with you. You read my story, so I won't bore you with the details you already know."

I told her I had read about the accident, the premature births, and that both the babies and the mother had pulled through. Her eyes suddenly opened wide and she had a strange grin on her face. I had the feeling that there was a lot more to this, and that it was going to sound just like what I had heard before—something unbelievable. It would turn out that my assumption was right on target.

The story she told me was both amazing and, if I had not already heard the accounts from the other reporters, unbelievable. The mother, near death, was rushed into the operating room. The doctors had little hope that she could be saved, and they decided to try to save the babies instead. The twins she was carrying were born weighing a little over a pound each, and they were immediately put on respirators. The mother flat-lined on the table as the doctors tried in vain to revive her. Then, once again, out of nowhere a man walked into the operating room and pushed the doctors aside with strength one of them described as beyond anything he had ever seen.

The stranger ran his hands over the woman's body and suddenly the heart monitor began to beep once again. She was not only alive, but every injury she had sustained had magically healed—even the C-section the doctors had performed to deliver her babies.

Then the man walked over to the babies and he ran his hand over them too. What had minutes before been two premature babies weighing just over a pound, were now two healthy babies weighing close to six pounds each.

Monica had her eyes fixed on me, anxious to see my reaction. When she did not see what she expected, she asked, "Why do I get the feeling that none of this surprises you in the least?"

I brushed off her question and asked one of my own. "How do you know all this?"

"Because I was there."

"You were there? You were in the operating room?"

"No," she replied. "I was at the hospital picking up a friend when all this happened."

"Did you see the man who did this?" I asked, though I was fairly certain I would get the same response as I had before, that he'd just disappeared.

"See him? Yes, I saw him *and* I talked to him. Why do you think I was so eager to meet with you?"

I wasn't sure exactly what she was talking about or, for that matter, what she thought I had to do with her conversation with the mystery man. "I am not sure I follow you, Monica."

"You don't know?" she asked me, looking about as puzzled as I felt.

"No, I have no idea."

"Well then, I wonder why he told me to come and see you."

"Come and see me? What do you mean by that?" I heard myself ask the question, but I was not completely sure I wanted to know the answer.

"He told me that a man was going to be contacting me to inquire about the story I wrote. He said it was very important that I tell this man everything I knew. I didn't know it was going to be you who would be contacting me, but when I received your e-mail, I knew I had to honor his request."

"Was that all he said to you?"

"No, he said he knew you were going to come looking for him, and it was fine with him. He said the time has come."

If she didn't see the look of shock, fear, and amazement in my expression earlier, she was certainly seeing it now. It took me a long moment to compose myself. I had an eerie feeling and began to look around the café wondering if he was somehow watching me.

"What are you looking for?" Monica asked me. Once again, I brushed off her question— this time, because I was too vain to tell her I was seriously freaked out at the moment.

"'The time has come.' Do you know what he meant by that?" I asked.

"No, I figured you might know since he meant for you to get the message." I asked her if she could give me a detailed description of this man. She was more than willing to comply. I thanked her for coming to see me. As we were leaving, I asked her if there was anything else at all she could tell me. "Yes, one more thing. His name is Zack."

My head was in such a fog that I didn't even remember my drive home. I sat down on my couch, leaned my head back against the wall, and began to wonder what the hell I had gotten myself into. I knew now, without a doubt, that it was the same man in every article I had sitting on my desk. *Who are you, Zack?* I kept asking myself over and over, *And how do you know that I have been trying to find out about you?* I had even more questions and fewer answers, and the answers I did come up with began to make me question myself. If all of this were true, what kind of a man could do these things and why did he want me to come and find him? If he wanted to talk to me, then why didn't he just come to me? I knew at that moment I had two choices: either drop this whole thing, or do what Zack had asked me to do—go and find him. I think I already knew which choice I was going to make.

Before I knew it, the day had passed and I had to get ready to meet Julie for dinner. Julie and I had been seeing each other for about a year. She was an attorney, a very good attorney. She had successfully argued two cases before the Supreme Court before she was thirty. She was now thirty-seven and I think she was beginning to get a little impatient with me. I was married once, for a year, six years ago. It was great for about two mouths, a living hell for five months, and very expensive to get out of. I was not in any hurry to try it again.

I met Julie at 7:30 at Morton's in Georgetown. As always, she looked beautiful, but then again Julie was one of those women who could look beautiful covered in mud. I know what you're thinking. I must be crazy. She's smart, beautiful and successful—what more could a guy want? In my case, it was my freedom.

We sat at the bar and ordered drinks while we waited for our table. Vodka on the rocks for me, white wine for Julie. I finished my first drink in record time and ordered another. "What's wrong, Michael? I've never seen you have two drinks before dinner."

I knew I had to tell her everything that had occurred since I started this, and I had avoided doing so when we talked during the week. But

I didn't think a crowded bar was the place to discuss it. I told her that I needed to discuss something with her, but I wanted to wait until we were seated. Julie gave me that raised-eyebrow look, but she did not press the issue any further while we were at the bar. The extra minutes gave me some more time to come up with exactly how I was going to spring all this on her.

Once we were seated, I waited until the waiter had done the usual show-and-tell. In the case of this restaurant, that meant that the waiter would bring out a fancy tray with all the prime cuts of meat neatly displayed for our selection. We placed our order of steak for me and a three-pound lobster for Julie.

I could tell Julie was getting anxious, so I began to tell her every last detail of what I had uncovered. That included my meeting with Monica and the message Zack had given her for me. I tried to get some idea of what Julie was thinking by watching her expression, but she just sat there staring at me the whole time. When I was finished, I must say her reaction truly surprised me. I expected her to go off on a tangent about how crazy this whole thing sounded, but she had the exact opposite response.

"My God, Michael, who do you think this Zack is?"

"I really don't know, Julie, and I have to say that part of me is scared to death to find out."

"You have to go and find this man. This could be the most amazing story of your career."

For a moment, I sat there wondering who the hell I was having dinner with. Julie was the biggest skeptic I had ever met. Now, suddenly she was a believer without even questioning whether any of this was true.

"First of all, I don't know how to find him even if I wanted to," I told her. "Secondly, why does he want me to come and look for him? If he wants to talk to me, it's certainly easy enough for him to find me."

That turned out to be the wrong thing to say because as soon as those words came out of my mouth, I got a fifteen-minute lecture about why a man like *that* does not come to you, you go to *him*.

Of course, Julie threw in a few bits about how I always told her that I wanted to someday write a story that would change the way the world looked at things, and this might just be that story. For good measure, she decided to throw in the fact that I might be too lazy to realize that dream.

She did know how to push my buttons, and she knew the "lazy" comment would push me over the edge. I may be a lot of things, but lazy is not one of them. "Okay, Julie, I'll go find him, but just remember that you wanted me to do this. I have no idea how long it will take, but you know once I start, I am not going to stop."

"I know you won't, that's what I love about you—you never give up until you get what you go after." Julie's words came with a smile that I had not seen in quite some time. I think somehow she knew that what I was about to do was going to change me forever. Somewhere deep down inside, I must have known it too. I raised my water glass to make a toast. "To Zack. Whoever or whatever you are, I accept your invitation. I'll see you soon."

Julie countered with her own toast. "To Zack. I hope you are as wonderful as you sound."

We finished dinner and went back to my townhouse where I showed Julie all the information I had compiled. We had a nightcap before going to bed and making love like we were a couple of teenagers. I suppose it must have been the excitement of the adventure ahead that fueled us, or maybe we both knew that it would be a while before we would see each other again. I slept soundly that night, holding Julie close to me for most of it.

I awoke the next morning with Julie's hair splayed across my face. I could smell the shampoo she had used. Normally I would have brushed her hair away, but I this morning I just wanted to take in that smell and etch it in my memory, to lie there with her and enjoy the moment. I started to think that maybe I was a bit more of a romantic than I realized.

When we did finally get out of bed, we were both silent. Julie showered and dressed while I made coffee. She broke the silence, asking me when I was planning to leave. I have to admit I really had not thought this through. I have no idea why I answered her the way I did—it just came out. "I am hoping to leave tomorrow. I just need to tie up a few loose ends before I leave."

Julie walked over and put her arms around me, kissing my right cheek. "So, am I one of those loose ends?" she whispered in my ear.

I reached down and grabbed her butt and told her with my best attempt at a devilish smile, "there is nothing loose about this end, sweetheart."

In reality, I did need her to help with a lot of the loose ends. I asked her to take care of things for me while I was gone, and she readily agreed. I needed someone to pay the bills in my absence, and she had done this for me previously when I was off chasing one story or another.

She smiled and put her hand on my chest. "I know this is going to sound crazy, but I am really proud of you right now."

"Why?" I asked her, thinking I just should have accepted the compliment and kept my mouth shut.

"I just have this feeling that you are about to do something pretty remarkable," she told me. "I know you don't like to talk about this, but I do love you. You're my best friend and you make me laugh even when I don't want to. I'm going to miss you even though you're the most stubborn man I have ever known."

I knew she was waiting for me to say something. For the first time, I realized just how important she was to me and how much I cared for her. Oh hell, I loved her, and I had been holding off from saying it for a long time. I figured that once I told her, the rings would not be far behind. I knew it was time to tell her, and the words came out far easier than I ever thought they would. "I love you too, Julie. I should have told you a long time ago and I know my silence has hurt you. For that I am sorry." She put her fingers over my lips and I could see the tears begin to well in her eyes.

"You told me now," she said, wrapping her arms around me and kissing me. I could taste her tears as they flowed down her face. Julie pulled back and smacked me playfully on the chest. "What the hell took you so long?"

We both laughed and I gave the best comeback I could think of. "I'm a little slow, but I get there eventually."

She smiled and pinched my cheek. "Yes, you do."

Julie and I went to breakfast and I bounced my plan off her for tracking down Zack. I would have my researchers continue to look for stories that sounded like they could be about Zack. I would try and get a fix on where he might be headed next and hope, at some point, to catch up to him. We both agreed that though it was probably not the surest plan, it was the only one either of us could come up with. I guess I was hoping that once I started looking for him, he would somehow know, just like he knew I was gathering information about him, and he would find me. It was not the most realistic of thoughts, but then again there was not that much about any of this that was remotely realistic. In all reality, I thought to myself, I had no idea where to even start looking. I hadn't exactly thought this through. For the first time in my career, I was going in search of a story without any certainty about what would be revealed.

I knew one thing for certain: I had to get started right away, before my more rational side began to make me realize just how crazy this whole idea was. I began to run through a mental list of what I would need to do before I left and what I would need to bring with me. I guess I was as ready as I was ever going to be.

It was Monday, January 25, 2010. This would be my last day in D.C. before I left to go in search of Zack. I had managed to get all of my affairs in order. I was fairly certain that I would be able to find Zack, get my interview, and be back home in less than thirty days. After all, he was expecting me. I didn't think there would be any problem getting him to agree to tell me about himself and what he was doing and, more importantly, how he was doing it. I had contacted my researchers and asked them to find the most recent story that was similar to the ones they had gathered for me two weeks ago. I also asked them to keep me posted through daily e-mails on anything new they discovered. I had a feeling Zack did not stay in one place for very long, and I was going to be doing a lot of traveling.

I called Al to tell him my plans and that I would not be available for our weekly dinners for a while. I was not surprised to find that Al was supportive of my quest. He not only wished me luck, but offered his help if I should need it. I thanked him and I assured him that I'd keep in touch along the way. I started packing my bags. Julie had made me a list—God, that woman loves lists—just to make sure I didn't forget anything. I started reading aloud each item on the list as I packed it into my bags. I had plenty of clothes for both warm and cold weather. I packed my cameras, even though I was not sure he was going to let me take his picture, and enough audio cassettes to fill over a hundred hours. I wanted to be sure that I didn't miss anything he had to say.

It was close to four in the afternoon and I still hadn't heard from my researchers. I was getting a bit antsy. I needed a starting point and I was counting on them to find it for me. It was almost five when an e-mail came from the researchers. Enclosed were two stories from Nashville, Tennessee. After reading them both, I knew where I was going. I just hoped Zack was still there.

I called Julie and said only one word when she picked up the phone—Nashville. Julie responded by trying her best southern accent on me. "Good luck, my love. I'll be waiting right here for you when you come back." I laughed and promised to call as often as I could. I told her I would miss her and that I meant everything I'd said. I'm not sure if I said that to reassure her or myself. I was in new territory with her now, and I knew she was as aware of that as I was. She blew a kiss into the phone before she hung up and, I must admit I was surprised how good that made me feel. I suddenly began to wonder if I was finally growing up.

I spent the rest of the evening just sitting in front of the television. I needed to try to keep my mind off what had consumed my thoughts for the last two weeks. I switched the channels, watching one mindless show after another. It had been a long time since I had watched anything on television that was not news-related. I was quite disheartened to see what the networks were passing off as entertainment these days. It seemed almost every show involved some sort of reality TV. Well, I thought to myself, I guess it's cheaper than paying actors. It did make me wonder, though, what does it say about all of us if this is what we accept as entertainment? I'd finally had enough and went to bed.

I slept better than I had expected that night, and I awoke the next morning ready to go. I showered, had my two cups of coffee, got dressed, and packed my bags into my Audi A6. I took one last look around to make sure I didn't forget anything. I left a note for Julie in a place I knew she would find it when she stopped over. It would certainly not go down in the annals of romantic prose, but for a man like me who has always had a hard time expressing his emotions, it was something special, or at least I was hoping she thought so.

It was 7:00 a.m. when I put the key in the ignition. I pulled out of my garage to a cold D.C. morning and headed for the highway. Next stop Nashville, I thought to myself—until I looked down at the gas gauge. I laughed and thought, next stop a gas station. I filled the tank and headed south on I-95. It was 660 miles to Nashville. If I made good time, I would get there in just under twelve hours.

I was actually glad that I had a long drive ahead of me. I enjoyed driving, and for some reason I always did my best thinking behind the wheel. I had already booked a room at the downtown Sheraton for a week. Since I had never been to Nashville, I chose a hotel that seemed to be centrally located. I settled in for the long drive ahead, and began, once again, to run the events of the last couple of weeks through my mind. My first thoughts, much to my surprise, were about Julie. After my divorce, I promised myself that I'd never make the same mistake again. I valued my independence in both my work and my personal life above all else. I had become, of my own making, a man who rarely talked about his feelings, and I did my best not to show them. Before I met Julie, I managed to push away many women who I'm sure thought of me as an unfeeling and uncaring man. I wouldn't really have disagreed with their assessment of me.

For some reason that I reminded myself to ask her next time we were together, Julie never gave up on me. I think she saw through the rather large barrier I had surrounded myself with, to see the person I am on the inside. It was either that or she was totally out of her mind, I thought, laughing to myself. I decided it was the former and told myself what a lucky bastard I was.

My mind then turned to Zack. Even though I had dropped everything in my life to track him down, I still wasn't sure exactly how much of all this I could comprehend. No one can bring a person back from the dead or do any of the things that I was told this man was capable of doing. Was this just some giant hoax or—and I have to tell you, this thought scared me more than a little—could he really do these things? And if he could, who was he, and why hadn't anyone found out about him before now? Anyone who was able to do the things he could would have been front-page news on every newspaper in the world. I wondered what I would say to him when we finally met. Would he be forthcoming and answer all my questions? I wondered where he was from and about his family. Did he had brothers and sisters, and if he did, did they possess the same abilities as he? I then came back to reality and realized I had no idea where to look for Zack. I was not sure if he was even still in Nashville, and if he was, how I was going to track him down. I started to realize that I really had not planned this very well, and I was just going to have play it by ear. But I had one thing going for me: I had lived my whole life playing it by ear and had done just fine.

I arrived at the Sheraton hotel in Nashville at 6:30. I had found a convoy of friendly truckers and followed them down the whole way. For most of the trip, we were doing well beyond the speed limit. My first surprise in Nashville was how nice the hotel was. I was really not certain what to expect, but I certainly did not expect such opulent surroundings. There was even a revolving restaurant at the top of the building that allowed a nice panoramic view of the city.

I decided to go to my room and unpack before heading down to the bar for a drink and a bite to eat. I took my key and headed up to my room. When I opened the door, I received the second surprise since my arrival. I had booked a single room with a king-sized bed, and it had somehow turned into a very large suite. There was a large flower arrangement on the dining room table, with a card attached. At first I assumed it was from the management, a welcome-to-the-hotel sort of thing, so I didn't bother to read the card. I don't know why I always do this, but every time I check into a hotel I always walk through the room checking out every little thing. My surveying was interrupted by the bellman knocking on my door. He was friendly and courteous, and I tipped him fifteen dollars for which he thanked me three times.

I put my bags on the bed and began to unpack, then decided I had better call Julie first to let her know I that I made it here in one piece. There was a phone on the table where the flowers were, so I grabbed the note before I sat down to dial. The note and the flowers were from Julie. She wrote, "I thought you would have more room to pace back and forth in a suite. Best of luck in finding Zack. I love you and miss you already."

I probably should have called the minute I pulled in, I thought to myself as I dialed Julie's number. "You know you did not have to do this," I told her as soon as she picked up.

"Well I wanted you to be comfortable. I figured you'd be doing a lot of pacing and you would need the room."

"Thanks, and thanks for the flowers. They are beautiful," I told her—not that I cared that much for flowers.

"So what's your first move?" Julie asked.

"Well, first I'm going to unpack, and then I'm going to go get something to eat. After that, I think I'll just hit the sack."

"You watch out for those southern belles." Julie warned me jokingly.

"I will, honey," I told her in my best southern accent. "None of them could hold a candle to you, my love."

"Good answer. You're learning," Julie said, laughing the whole time. "Sleep well, Michael. I wish I were there with you."

"I love you."

"I love you too. Good night." And then I hung up the phone.

I unpacked the last suitcase and set up my laptop to check if I had any messages from my researchers. Unfortunately, there were none, but Al had left me a good-luck message repeating his offer of help should I need it. Talking to Julie had made me feel better about being here and what I was doing. I guess the fact that she was behind me on this meant more to me than I had anticipated. I wondered what I would have done if she had felt differently and had been opposed to me doing this. Would I have gone anyway? As much as I loved her, I knew the answer was yes. This is what I do. This is a part of who I am. I think she knows that as well as I do. That's just one of the many reasons I love her.

I went down to the bar located in the lobby. It was just as nice as the rest of the hotel, and I was surprised by how crowded it was. I managed to get a seat at the bar, a very large one, where there were two bartenders happily pouring drinks. Both were very attractive blondes who looked to be in their early thirties. The taller of the two came over and placed a coaster on the bar in front of me.

"What can I get for you, sir?" she asked me in one of those deep southern accents.

"I'll have a vodka on the rocks with a twist."

"Any particular type?"

"Vox, if you have it," I said, reminding myself that I was in unfamiliar territory and the bartenders didn't know me.

"Sure, we have it," she answered, walking away to get my drink. When she came back with it, I noticed her gold name tag said Sarah. I had already noticed there were other people eating at the bar, something for which I was thankful. I was not really in the mood to go into a restaurant and eat alone. "Is there anything else I can get for you sir?" Sarah asked.

"As a matter of fact, there is. Can I see a menu, please?" The bar menu was small, but I found something that suited me just fine. When Sarah came back over I ordered a cheeseburger and fries.

I was on my second vodka when my food arrived. They must have big appetites in Nashville because the cheeseburger was enormous and there were enough fries on there to feed three people. Sarah saw my expression. "I guess I should have told you how big they are."

"I don't know whether to eat this or use it as a Frisbee," I replied, trying my best to make a friendly joke.

"Enjoy!" Sarah told me before going back to her duties behind the bar.

It turns out I had more of an appetite than I thought, or maybe it was just that the burger was fantastic, but I ate almost everything on the plate. I ordered one more vodka and sat back in my seat and began to look around the room. The crowd seemed to be a mix of locals and hotel guests. Their attire ranged from business suits to sweatshirts. I probably could have struck up a conversation with several people, but I was not much in the mood for small talk. I finished my drink and motioned for Sarah to bring me my check.

"Are you a guest in the hotel?" Sarah asked.

"Yes," I told her. "But I'll pay cash." She gave me a smile and placed the check in front of me. It was only twenty-three dollars, quite a deal if you ask me. I laid two twenties on the bar and headed back up to my room.

When I got back to my room, I sat down on the couch and picked up the television remote. I thought I'd try and catch the local news. Who knows? Maybe I would see something that would give me a hint that Zack was still in town. I guess the drinks were running through me and I needed to hit the bathroom. Passing the bed on my way over, I noticed it had been turned down and there was a white envelope sitting on top of my pillow. I figured it was just a welcome note or one of those satisfaction surveys hotels like to ask you to fill out. I picked it up on my way back from the bathroom and laid it next to me on the couch. It was only 9:30, a little too early for the news, so I just sat there flipping through the channels. I settled on a show about the way dogs and man evolved together. What can I tell you? I was bored, and it turned out to be a fairly interesting program.

It was during one of the commercials that I glanced over at the envelope sitting next to me. I picked it up and pulled out the note inside. As soon as I saw what was written, I bolted straight up in my seat. If anyone had been there to see my face, I'm certain my expression would have been one of shock. It read: "I'm glad you decided to take me up on my offer and come and find me. You just sit tight. I will come to you when the time is right. In the meantime, take in some sights. There's a lot to see here. Oh by the way, nice flowers." It was signed *Zack*.

At that moment, you could have knocked me over with a feather. I just sat there not really sure how to react. How could he possibly know I was here and in this room? Was he in the bar? Did I see him and not even know it? Why is it that everything about this man is just one question after another, all of them with no answers?

I finally got up off the couch and started to look around my hotel wondering if he had been looking through my things while he was here. It did not look like anything had been touched, but I did have a strange feeling that my space had been violated.

I sat down on my bed and reached for the phone. I dialed Julie's number hoping that she was home. When she answered, I'm not even sure I said hello. I just started telling her what had happened. Julie had the same questions I did, but I could tell she was starting to worry about me. She kept reminding me of the fact that I really knew nothing about this man. She even theorized that he might not be the Good Samaritan that I had envisioned him to be. All of this, of course, merely added to the more than mild state of paranoia I found myself in. I used my better judgment and decided not to tell her that her words would probably keep me up all night. I knew she was just concerned about my safety and, at that moment, so was I. I managed to calm Julie down before I said goodnight and hung up the phone.

In the silence of my hotel room, I began to laugh quietly to myself. I came looking for this man because of the wonderful things he had done for complete strangers. There was nothing that indicated that he had done any harm to anyone. I was, in some small way, ashamed of the fact I had even thought he could or would cause me harm. Besides, if that was truly his intention, I doubt that I could do anything to stop him. I reread Zack's note and I wondered what he meant by "when the time is right." What time was he talking about? Did he mean that he had things to do before he was ready to talk to me? There I was with more questions. I decided to start writing down my thoughts and my questions, as I was not sure how much time I was going to be waiting for him or, for that matter, how much time he was going to give me to interview him.

I grabbed a note pad from my bag and began to compose my thoughts. Even as I was writing, I found myself mentally filling in the answers to my question, or should I say the answers that I was hoping he would give me. The truth is that I wanted him to be something special, something far beyond the rest of the human race. I realized that by building this man up in my mind, I was pretty much guaranteeing myself a letdown when the truth came out. But at that moment I was content with my thoughts and that was all that mattered. It had been a long day and I was beginning to feel it. I jumped into the shower and then got into bed. I normally take awhile to fall asleep, but not tonight. Strange bed and all, I was asleep within a few minutes.

I slept very well that night and awoke almost two hours later than I normally do. I showered, shaved, and even though I rarely have anything in the morning but a cup of coffee, I decided to treat myself and order breakfast through room service. I ordered bacon and eggs, a toasted bagel, orange juice, and a pot of coffee. It took less than twenty minutes for my feast to be delivered by another friendly and smiling hotel employee. I could get used to this kind of treatment, I thought to myself. I signed the bill and handed the young man a ten. He thanked me and promptly left me alone to eat my meal. I guess it must have been be the southern air because I finished every last bite and probably could have eaten more. Just after I put my plates back on the cart and wheeled it into the hallway for someone to pick up, my phone rang. I knew who it was even before I picked it up.

"Good morning." Julie's voice was far calmer than it was last night. "I just wanted to make sure you were still in one piece," she said with a bit of sarcasm in her voice.

"I'm fine, the bogeyman didn't get me," I told her.

"I'm sorry I got a little carried away last night," she said, this time with out the sarcastic tone. "I just can't figure this guy out, and you know how I am when it comes to that."

I knew all too well how Julie was. We were very different when it came to how we viewed people. Julie thought everyone had a motive for what they did. She believed that people always had an underlying reason for their actions. She had told me about a boyfriend she had years before who was quite fond of giving her gifts. She came to realize that one of the reasons he was so generous was because it made him happy to see her enjoy her gifts, so in a way his generosity was as much for his pleasure as it was for hers. I had always believed that people did things for many different reasons and often with no thought of how their actions would be perceived or rewarded. I had come to understand that she was a far more logical thinker than I was, but I never had a problem with that.

"I know, Julie, but I just don't think this guy thinks the way you do. Remember how I came to find out about him in the first place? If it hadn't been for the story I wanted to write, I would have never even have heard of him. How could he possibly have had some plan in mind for me when he didn't even know I would ever find out he existed?"

"Okay you're right," Julie fired back. "So what are you going to do now, just sit there and wait?"

"What choice do I have, Julie? I'm certainly not going to leave. Maybe he's testing me, trying to see just how interested in talking to him I really am."

Hearing those words come out of my mouth, I suddenly realized I sounded just like Julie. She did not let that get past her. "What was that?" she asked. "Now who's thinking he has a motive behind his actions?"

"Alright," I told her. "I have no idea why he wants me to stay put and wait for him to contact me. I only know this: if I want this interview—and believe me, I do—I am going to have to do this by his rules whatever the hell they might be. I'm going to stay here until he contacts me. I just hope it's sooner rather than later."

"I understand," Julie said. "I'm behind you on this one hundred percent. You be careful and stay in touch," she told me before we hung up.

I spent the next four days in Nashville trying to keep myself occupied. I tried my best, but I was never much for sightseeing so I bought a few books and magazines to keep my mind busy. I spoke with Julie twice a day, giving her a full report of my, so far, uneventful time.

By the time Saturday night came, I was getting a little stir crazy. My hotel suite, which felt so spacious when I first arrived, was now feeling like a closet. It was around ten o'clock when I finally decided to go out and get some fresh air. I grabbed my coat and headed down the elevator to the lobby. I walked out through the front doors, looked to my left, then to my right. I had no idea which way to go, so I turned to my right and started walking. It was not as cold as it would be in D.C. on a late January night, but it was still quite brisk. After about an hour of walking, I came upon Lucky's Tavern. I probably should have walked in a straight line when I left the hotel, but I didn't and I wasn't quite sure I could find my way back that easily. I decided to head into Lucky's for a drink and then call a cab to take me back to the hotel.

Lucky's seemed like one of those neighborhood bars, the kind of place you would frequent to if you lived in the area, but probably would not make a special trip to visit. The bar was long and there were pictures of sports figures all over the walls. There were a couple of pool tables at the back of the room, each being used by two or more players. It was not that crowded and I found myself a seat at the bar, fairly close to the front door.

The bartender was talking to two good-looking women at the bar, and it took him a few minutes to even notice I had sat down. He was tall and stocky and looked to be in his late twenties. "What can I get for you?" he asked when he was finally able to tear himself away from the two women he had been talking to.

"I'll have a vodka on the rocks with a twist," I replied, not bothering to ask for a brand. He brought my drink quickly and I just sat there, not sure if I wanted the drink or a cab ride back to my hotel. My thoughts were suddenly interrupted by a loud noise behind me. I turned around to see that it was coming from four men who had just entered the tavern.

They looked like they had already had plenty to drink. They were young, not much past twenty-one, and they were having a hard time even walking in a straight line. I thought for certain the bartender would notice how intoxicated they were and refuse to serve them any more alcohol. One of them staggered up to the bar and yelled, "hey, Jack, we need some drinks over here!" The bartender grabbed four bottles of beer and brought them right over. I assumed they must be regulars. I guess I could understand. More times than I cared to remember, bartenders I knew had served me when we both knew I had had enough.

I went back to my drink and my thoughts. I felt a blast of cold air behind me from the opening of the front door, and before I could turn around I heard a woman's voice. "Is anyone sitting here?" she asked me in a very deep southern accent. As I turned around, I could see that the voice came from a very beautiful blond.

"No," I told her. "Please have a seat." She immediately sat down next to me.

"You're not from around here, are you?" she questioned.

"Is it that obvious?"

"Well," she said. "You have a northern accent and you're a little over-dressed for a place like this. Not too many cashmere overcoats in here." She smiled.

The bartender wasted no time in coming over this time. I guess if you wanted quick service in here, you needed to be an attractive woman. Apparently, the bartender was not the only one to notice the beauty sitting on my left. The four intoxicated young men must have gotten a good look at her when she came in. The next thing I knew, the four of them were surrounding us at the bar. At first, they didn't acknowledge my presence. They seemed quite content to just try and make small talk with the young lady. Then, suddenly, one of them put a hand on my shoulder. "Hey, old man, why don't you go sit somewhere else?" I looked back at the one who was talking to me. He stunk of beer and his eyelids were half closed.

"I'm just going to finish my drink and then I'm out of here," I told him, thinking that the fact I was planning to leave soon would be enough to satisfy him. I was wrong. He grabbed me again, and this time, spun me around in my chair so I was facing him and his friends.

"I told you to get the fuck out of the chair before I throw you off it." He was about my size, and very drunk, and if he didn't have four friends with him I probably would have had little trouble handling him. I was a Golden Glove boxer when I was younger and had kept myself in very good shape through the years, but my better judgment told me it was time to go. Before I could get up, his friend quickly started to get in on the act. "Let's kick his ass," he bellowed. The bartender suddenly came over. For a moment I thought I might be getting a little help, but that didn't turn out to be the case.

"Hey, you want to fuck this guy up, do it outside," he told them.

Just as I thought I was in for a beating, I heard another voice from my left. "I think you boys should stick to your drinking. It will be a lot safer for you that way." The man put his hand on my shoulder and just nodded like he knew me. He was well over six feet tall and built like an athlete. He had brown hair and eyes and he was wearing a Grateful Dead baseball cap. He spoke without an accent of any kind, so I assumed that, like me, he was not a local.

"Mind your own fucking business, dickhead," the one who had originally grabbed me yelled at him.

"Why, so the four of you can gang up on this guy? And I really do not like being called a dickhead," my new friend spoke back at him with anger in his voice.

I guess that was enough to set off the drunk who grabbed me. He took a swing at the guy who had come to my defense. It would turn out to be the worst thing he could have done. His fist never made its target. The man in the Grateful Dead hat caught his fist in his right hand and just held it there for a moment. With his other hand he grabbed the drunk by the front of his shirt and threw him against the back wall of the bar some sixty feet away. He slammed into the wall so hard he knocked most of the pictures right off the wall. "I told you I didn't like being called a dickhead," he said with a cocked smile on his face.

For a moment, like me and everyone else in the bar, his three friends just stared with a look of shock on their faces. Then the largest of the three still standing screamed, "I'm going to kick your ass." It was the last thing he would say, at least for awhile. The man in the cap threw the three of them around that bar like they were paper dolls. They didn't stand a chance against this man. When it was over, the four of them were left on the floor moaning in pain. I guess the bartender did not like to see his regulars get beaten up so badly. He reached for a baseball bat from under the bar. Before he even had the chance to swing it, the man grabbed it from his hands, broke it in three places like it was a twig, and dropped it on the floor.

The bartender raised both hands in the air as a sign of surrender. As I glanced around the rest of the tavern, everyone else seemed to be taking the bartender's lead. They were all standing against the walls, some with their hands in the air. The man in the cap turned to look at the bartender. "Are these idiots friends of yours?" he asked. The bartender nodded. "Then I suggest you call a couple of ambulances. They are going to need a long hospital stay. Oh, one more thing—it's not that smart to serve drunks."

I stood up and walked over to this man, my arm extended to shake his hand. "I don't know how to thank you," I said to him.

"I told you to see some sites, Michael, not get buried under one of them," he said with a big smile on his face.

"Zack?"

32

"Who the hell else knows you're here?" He shook his head. "Yes. Zackary Breeze. It's a pleasure to meet you," he said as he shook my hand. "I think we've worn out our welcome here, Michael. Let's get out of here."

"Sure," I said, following him out the front door. I was still very shaken up by what I had just witnessed, but I would not have believed what had just happened had I not witnessed it myself. I literally watched a man throw a 200-pounder sixty feet across the room with one hand and seemingly no effort at all. I could not imagine a human being could be that strong. At that moment I was not sure exactly who or what was standing next to me.

"So, are you enjoying your stay in Nashville?" Zack asked once again with a big smile on his face.

"I have to ask you," I replied. "How the hell did you do that?"

"Do what?"

"You know what I mean. You threw those guys around like they were dish towels."

"I'll tell you what. Why don't we just enjoy the night air. There will be plenty of time for all your questions." I had a feeling those were the last words I was going to get out of him for now, so I just walked along beside him.

I may have been keeping my mouth shut, but my mind has whirling. I found it perplexing that I had come to know of Zack because of the people he had rescued from harm, and tonight I saw him do just the opposite. He did not really seem to care how badly he had hurt those young men from the bar. I wondered why that surprised me. Had I put undue expectations on him thinking that he was here to do only what I considered good deeds? Had it had been anyone else in that situation, would they care what happened to someone who was trying to attack them? I really wanted to get some answers from him. I had a hard time keeping myself from blurting out my thoughts as we walked.

33

It was about half an hour before we turned a corner and I saw my hotel. We walked into the lobby together, and Zack decided that the time for silence was over. "I'll pick you up right outside tomorrow morning at ten."

"Alright. Where are we going?"

"You'll find out in the morning," Zack replied. "Make sure your bags are packed and you're checked out of your room."

"My bags? So we're leaving Nashville?"

"That's right, we're leaving. Go on, get some rest," Zack said as he turned to leave the hotel.

"Thanks again for what you did tonight," I said to his back as he walked away.

"No problem." And he turned back to me for a moment before he walked out of the hotel.

Julie is not going to believe this, I thought to myself as I rode up the elevator to my floor. When the elevator door opened, I ran down the hallway like a kid, my adrenaline pumping through me like never before. I had been excited about stories I had done before, but this was different. I knew now that Zack was unlike anyone I had ever before come into contact with. I knew that this would be the most remarkable story I was ever going to come across. I had no idea why I was so certain of this, but I knew I was about to find out. I called Julie as soon as I walked into my room. I told her the whole story and that Zack and I were leaving Nashville tomorrow. I had a feeling that Julie might be a little troubled with the fact that I was leaving tomorrow morning with a man I had only met the night before, but once again I was wrong. She was almost as excited about this as I was. She told me to be careful and to keep in touch and stay out of trouble. I promised I would and I told her I loved her very much. Julie replied in kind and I hung up the phone.

I went into the bathroom to brush my teeth and get ready for bed and suddenly it dawned on me—Julie never asked where we were going. Even stranger was that I never asked Zack either. I guess I'd find that out tomorrow morning.

I decided to pack my bags before I went to bed. I was still pretty pumped up and needed to do something. When I was through packing, I started jotting down more questions for Zack. I was hoping he would be more talkative in the morning and if he was, I wanted to be ready. I did not fall asleep until almost one in the morning and I was glad I left an 8:30 wake-up call because it was the sound of the phone that woke me from a very deep sleep.

I remembered that they had coffee every morning in the lobby, and I decided that I would take advantage of that perk. I did not want to risk ordering room service as it might make me late in meeting Zack. I showered, shaved, and called the bell captain to come for my bags. By the time I finished checking out and grabbing a cup of coffee, it was about 9:15. I sat there in one of the comfortable chairs in the lobby that faced the front door waiting anxiously for ten o'clock.

Suddenly, I remembered my car was still in the hotel parking garage. I reached for my cell phone and called Julie. I knew her firm had an office here in Nashville. I asked if she could possibly have someone from that office come by here and pick up my car. Julie put me on hold to call her Nashville office while I walked over to the concierge to make sure they were okay with someone else picking up my car. The concierge was only too happy to oblige and I gave him my keys, my parking ticket, and a fifty-dollar bill. Julie came back on the line and told me that it was all handled. Someone would be there within the next two hours. I asked the concierge if he would be here for the next few hours and he told me he would. I gave his name to Julie and told her to tell whoever was picking up the car to ask for the concierge by name. Julie had to run. She wished me luck once again before the line went dead. I thanked the concierge, making sure to tell him how accommodating everyone had been during my stay here. I then went back to my chair to finish my coffee.

It was five minutes to ten when I walked through the lobby doors dragging my three bags along with me. "Do you need a cab sir?" the doorman asked me as soon as I stepped outside.

"No, thank you, I'm waiting for someone." As soon as I spoke those words, the thought *I hope I am waiting for someone* came to my mind. Before I even had the chance to think any more about it, a big black Lexus SUV pulled up in front of the hotel. It was Zack. He stopped the vehicle, got out, and reached his arm out to shake my hand.

"You ready?" He asked.

"I'm ready."

Zack walked around to the back of the truck and opened the back hatch. "I see you don't travel light," he said, looking down at my three bags.

"I like to be prepared. You never know what you might need."

"Okay, Boy Scout," he said, closing the hatch after I threw my bags back there.

I walked over, opened the passenger-side door, and climbed in. Zack was inside a moment after me and we were on our way. I was still wary about starting to ask questions. I somehow had the feeling that I needed to wait for Zack to let me know when he was ready to talk. It turned out I did not have to wait very long.

"So why did you decide to come and look for me?"

I did not know at that point that it was never my decision. "I wanted to know if you were for real." It was the first thought that came to my mind, not exactly a great response.

"For real," Zack answered, laughing. "I guess you already answered that one, so now you can go on home."

Oh shit, I thought, did I just screw this up? Before I could think of some way to get my foot out of my mouth, Zack started laughing. "I'm just joking with you, Michael. Chill out."

"Alright, I'm chilled. I'm here to find out about you. I read a lot of stories about the things you did for people, and I want to know how you do the things you do. I was hoping you'd let me interview you."

"I guess we need to get something straight right off the bat, Michael. I did not invite you here so you could come and interview me for a few hours and leave."

"Then why did you bring me here?" I asked, not completely sure I wanted to know the answer.

"I brought you here to write about what we're going to do together. If you want this story, you're going to be here to live it. I want you to write what you see and what I'm trying to do, and that's going to take time. Think months, Michael, not hours. If you're not prepared to do this, tell me now and I'll take you back to your hotel."

I must admit I did have a brief moment when I thought I'd ask Zack to take me back to the hotel, but it quickly passed. I was still not sure who he was or how he could do the things he did, but I knew I was not going home until I got what I came for. "I'm in, Zack, however long it takes."

"I'm glad to hear that. I think we're going to make a good team, Michael. You've got guts. I admire that."

"Thanks, Zack, I'll try my best to write the finest story I can."

"All you need to do is write the truth, Michael, the rest will fall into place."

"Zack, exactly what are we going to be doing?"

"Let's put it this way—we're going to change the world."

I heard his words and I realized that as crazy as it sounded, I believed him. Somehow I knew that he could actually do what he said. Maybe it was really me who was crazy.

I had no idea where we were headed at that point, and it was not really that important. I came to realize that my part in all this was going to be to chronicle all of the actions of this man sitting next to me. I was just along for the ride, so I was just going to sit back and wait for something to happen.

We were heading south on I-95 and after about three hours on the road, Zack decided to pull off the highway. We ended up parked in front of a diner somewhere in the middle of nowhere. I was not even sure what state we were in. We went in and the waitress sat us down in the last booth in the back of the diner. I looked around the place as we walked through, partly because I was curious, and partly because I wanted to see if it looked clean enough to eat something. It was fairly crowded. At the far corner sat a family who could barely speak English. They were trying to place their order. I finally determined they were speaking German. "I think those people are having a hard time getting the waitress to understand them," I said to Zack. Zack got up and walked over to them. I followed along behind him, not sure what he was doing.

Zack began to speak to them in fluent German, translating everything to the waitress. They were a young couple with two daughters who both looked to be no older than six or seven. They were quite grateful that Zack was translating, and the father shook Zack's hand when he was through. We went back to our seats.

"So you speak German?" I asked.

"No, not really. I know a few words," he said with a smile I would soon come to recognize meant we were not going to talk any further about a subject. The waitress came over and took our order. We both went with the cheeseburger special and an iced tea. Our food arrived quickly and I dug right in. I had really not eaten anything all day and I was pretty hungry.

I was almost finished when I noticed Zack had barely touched his food. He was preoccupied with something going on at the other end of the diner. I looked back over my shoulder trying to see what he was looking at. There were three men sitting at the counter which ran parallel to the booths down the entire length of the diner. They were sitting right across from the family that Zack had translated for. I could see that they were turning around to say something to the family, but I was not able to hear. Still, I could tell from the expressions on their faces that whatever it was, it was not nice. Then one of them opened a saltshaker, poured the salt in his hands, and threw it over toward them in the direction of the two children. Zack stood up. I looked at his face and it was not hard to see that he was angry.

He walked over to the family and spoke to them in German. I assumed he was trying to find out what happened. The two little girls were crying and their mother was trying her best to calm them down. They had already finished their meal, and Zack must have told them to leave because they got up and began to walk out of the diner. At first, the three men seemed not to even notice that Zack had walked them out. They just sat there at the counter, not saying a word. But then one of them stood up and the other two followed his lead. I followed the three of them out of the diner. By the time I got there, the family was already in their car. Zack was leaning into the driver-side window talking to the father.

Zack stood up and tapped the roof of the car, then watched them pull away. When they were just about out of sight, he turned around back toward the diner. The three men who had been bothering the family were standing there a short distance in front of him. Zack started to walk toward the men, each of whom had at least fifty pounds on him.

"I guess you guys must be pretty proud of yourselves," Zack said to them. "You managed to scare a four- and a six-year-old to death." The three of them looked at each other, trying to decide which one was going to get the pleasure of trying to hurt Zack. I looked over at the diner and saw everyone in there was now looking out the windows. I guess they knew something was going to happen when the three men followed Zack outside. Suddenly, the largest of the three began to move menacingly toward Zack. He cocked his right arm back, his hand clenched in a fist. Before he even had a chance to throw a punch, Zack slapped him with his left hand. His slap had such force it lifted the man off his feet, spun him around in the air twice, and left him lying on the ground, sprawled out and unconscious.

The other two just stood there with looks of disbelief on their faces. Zack looked over at them. "So what's wrong, boys? Are you just a couple of pussies? Or do you only pick on little girls?" With that, the other two ran toward their pick-up truck. Zack did not pursue them, he just let them go. I watched them speed away, leaving their friend lying on the ground.

Zack walked back into the diner, sat back down, and finished his meal. Everyone stared at him, not saying a word. When we asked for the check, the waitress told us it was on the house. I reached into my pocket and put twenty-five dollars on the table. Zack acknowledged my gesture with a nod, and we headed for the front door. We walked out into the parking lot right past the man still lying on the ground. I looked back at him one more time before I climbed into the passenger seat. I was beginning to wonder if he was seriously hurt.

"Zack, you think he's going to be okay?"

"He'll be fine, Michael. I just hope he learned a lesson today. I realize you've seen me resort to violence twice since we met. I really don't like to hurt people, and I will almost never initiate violence. But I will always respond when someone attacks me."

I thought hard on his words, and I wrote them down in one of the notebooks I had brought with me. Well, I now know that he speaks German, and with a swipe of his hand, he can knock a 300-pound man off his feet and spin him around like a top. It would also seem that he has a problem with people who pick on children. It was not much, but it had only been a few hours since our journey began.

We kept driving for the next few hours, and after watching the road signs, I realized we were now in Georgia. We were about sixty miles outside of Atlanta when Zack pulled off the road into the parking lot of the Regency hotel. I had never heard of this hotel before, and I later found out it was a small chain of semi-luxury hotels that operated in three southern states. Zack checked us in to a two-bedroom suite and we headed up to our room. "I'm going to take a shower and change before dinner, Michael. Why don't you call Julie and let her know you're still in one piece?" He smiled at me and walked into one of the bedrooms, closing the door behind him.

I walked over to the phone and dialed Julie's number. She was not home, so I left a message on her voice-mail. I decided it was best just to tell her where I was and that I was okay. I didn't think it was the right time to go into too much detail like the fact that I had no idea how long I was going to be gone, or that I had seen Zack kick the crap out of someone else today. That conversation would have to come later.

I walked into my bedroom, threw my bags on the bed, and went into the bathroom to shower. By the time I was done and walked out to the living room area, Zack was already there sitting on the couch in front on the television. I had not really noticed Zack's appearance until now, but I finally took a good look at him. He had dark brown, wavy hair that almost covered his ears. It was longer in the back coming down to below his collar. At first glance, there was nothing that special about him. He was a nice looking guy, but as I looked closer, I noticed he did not have a single imperfection in his face. Everyone I had ever come in contact with had something—a scar, a pock-mark, an indentation, something—but not Zack. I was not sure that this was of any importance, but I filed it away in my mind just the same.

Zack seemed very interested in what he was watching on the television. I came around to see what had him so engrossed. It was a human-interest segment from the Atlanta news channel. The story was about a seven-year-old black girl who had contracted HIV from a blood transfusion. She was giving an interview to one of the local reporters. As I listened to this seven-year-old talk, I, too, was engrossed in her story. She was talking frankly and bravely about her own impending death. She was a patient in the children's AIDS ward at Atlanta General Hospital. She spoke of the other children in the ward and how unfair it was that they were all going to die at such an early age. I had covered many stories during wartime and had been on the front lines with soldiers who would soon be going into battle, but as I watched this little girl speak, I realized I had never seen such courage before.

Zack's eyes never left the screen as he took in every word she uttered. I watched his face as he listened to her doctors and then to her parents, who could hardly hold back their tears as they were being interviewed. At the end of the story, I heard them mention her name. It was Domenique Williams. Zack turned the television off and looked over at me.

"That is one brave little girl," I said to him.

"Yes she is," Zack said. "Yes she is."

Zack stood up and we headed downstairs to what turned out to be a very nice seafood and steak restaurant. Once we were seated and had placed our orders, I decided to see if I could get Zack to at least give me a little background information. I had brought a micro-cassette recorder downstairs with me just in case I was able to get him talking.

"So, Zack, where are you from?" I asked the question as I hit the record button on the machine and looked toward him for approval. He did not seem to mind that I had turned the machine on.

"I'm from a little town outside Philadelphia called Bala Cynwyd."

"Does your family still live there?" I asked, hoping to keep him talking.

"Yes, they do," he replied.

"Do you have any brothers or sisters?" I kept the questions coming. This was as talkative as he'd been since I'd met him.

"Yes, I have five brothers. I am the youngest."

"How old are you?"

"I'm forty-one," he replied.

I looked at him once again. Forty-one, I thought to myself. He was only a few years younger than I was, but he looked like he was barely over thirty.

"Does your family know where you are and what you've been doing?" Even as I asked the question, I wondered if I was pushing too hard. I didn't want him to stop talking now that I had gotten him started.

"Yes, they know, and yes, they know about what I'm doing. Before I left home, I told them all."

"So what exactly are you doing?" Just as I was finishing my question, the waiter brought our food to the table.

"That's enough talk for tonight, Michael. It's time to eat. We have someone to go see tomorrow."

"Who?"

"Domenique Williams," he said, as he started to eat his meal. We finished our meal which, by the way, turned out to be quite good, and we went back up to the room.

"So, Zack, when are you really going to start talking to me? Isn't that what I'm here for?" I asked him.

"Michael, believe me, before long you will be tired of hearing my voice, but for now I think it is better that you just watch. I know that might be a little tough for you, but bear with me. You will not have much longer to wait."

"Alright, Zack, I'll do my best to keep the questions at a minimum."

I watched him head toward the door to his bedroom. He turned back just before he walked into the room. "Goodnight, Michael. I'll see you in the morning. Oh, and tell Julie I said hello, and I look forward to meeting her someday."

"Goodnight, Zack," I replied. He closed the door to his bedroom.

I headed into my bedroom, picked up the phone that was on the night-stand next to the bed, and dialed Julie's number. I was still not sure how much I was going to tell her of what transpired today, but it did make me feel good to hear her voice on the other end of the line.

"Hi, sweetheart," I said to her.

"Is everything okay?" she asked.

"Yes, everything is fine. I'm okay."

"So, what's he like?" Julie asked.

"Well, he seems to be a nice guy. He doesn't talk that much about himself," I told her.

"So, how are you supposed to interview him if he doesn't want to talk about himself?"

I should have known that she would ask that. Now I'm going to have to tell her what Zack wants of me. I decided to just come clean. I told Julie everything that had happened that day and I waited for her to erupt. I was once again surprised by her response. "Michael, I trust your instincts. If you think this is the right thing to do, then you have to see it through."

"It's hard to explain, Julie, but I do have to do this. I know that I need to earn his trust, and I don't know how long that's going to take. I know there's something special about him. I sense it, but I just can't figure out what it is. I know if he wanted to, he could break me in two, but I have absolutely no fear of him whatsoever."

"So, did he tell you why you are going to see that little girl tomorrow?" Julie asked.

"No, he didn't," I replied, wondering the same thing myself.

"She has HIV, right?"

"Yes," I told her.

"Do you think that he's going there to cure her like he did with those other people?"

"I guess it's a possibility, but I have a feeling he might have something else in mind. Please don't ask me what that is because I have no clue."

"Just promise me you won't try to be a hero while you're out there with him."

"I promise, Julie. I'd better try and get some sleep. I have no idea how early we're going to be leaving tomorrow. By the way, Zack said he's looking forward to meeting you someday."

"You tell him the feeling is mutual, Michael, and tell him to keep you safe."

We both said our goodnights and I hung up the phone. I decided to get into bed. It was only ten o'clock, a little earlier than I usually went to bed, but I turned out the lights hoping that sleep would come quickly as I anticipated what the next day would bring. I was lucky. Within ten minutes, I was fast asleep.

I awoke the next morning at around quarter to six to find Zack standing over me, completely dressed. "I told you we were going to get an early start, didn't I?" Zack said.

"Yes, you did, but you never told me how early," I snapped back at him. "Maybe if you talked a little more, I'd know when the hell to get up." Zack just started laughing.

"When you're right, you're right," he said. "Go jump in the shower. I ordered room service and it should be here by the time you get out."

Zack walked out of the room and closed the door behind him. I slowly got up from the bed and headed into the shower. The warm water bought me back to life. I shaved and dressed and just as Zack predicted, by the time I got out to the main room, breakfast was there waiting. "I wasn't sure what you liked to eat in the morning Michael, so I got a little bit of everything."

I walked over the cart and saw he wasn't kidding. It was full of plates, each with a warming top. I began to open up the tops to see what was under them. There was everything from eggs Benedict to pancakes. There was coffee, tea, and various types of fruit. I thought to myself, this guy does not do anything small. I decided on coffee, eggs Benedict, and a bowl of fruit. We finished our breakfast and headed down to the lobby to check out. I offered to pay for the room, but Zack would not let me. He would not even let me split it with him. I reluctantly gave in, but not without letting him know that I was used to paying my own way.

We left the hotel a little after nine and we were once again on the road. This time at least I knew where we were going. I had been to Atlanta once before, many years ago. It was only for a couple of days, and I had little memory of the city. One thing I surely did not remember was the amount of traffic. It was even worse than the traffic around D.C.

We were on the road almost two and a half hours before we pulled into the parking garage of the hospital. Before we got out of the car, Zack reached behind my seat and pulled a red cap from the storage holder and put it on. The front of the cap had the prancing horse symbol that Ferrari had made famous. I followed Zack as he made his way through the hospital.

He seemed to know exactly where he was going, so much so that at one point I asked him if he had ever been there before. He told me he had not.

Somehow that did not surprise me.

When we arrived at the children's ward, I saw a young black couple standing at the nurses' station. They were with three people: two men and one woman, all dressed in hospital attire. The young black woman turned and when she saw Zack and me coming toward her, her eyes opened wide and she gasped as she held her hand over her mouth. With her other hand, she motioned for the man next to her to look toward us. His reaction was almost the same as hers. He looked shocked to see us. Zack walked up to the young couple and said, "Mr. and Mrs. Williams, my name is Zackary Breeze." They both just stood there for a moment looking at the two of us, but mostly they were looking at Zack.

"Our daughter told us you would be coming here today," Mr. Williams replied. "She said you spoke to her in a dream. She even described the clothes you would be wearing. How could that be? How could she know that you were coming here?"

I think at that moment I was just as shocked as James and Melody Williams were. How could Domenique have known that we were coming here today? My first thought was that Zack must have called her on the phone, but that would turn out not to be the case. "Mr. and Mrs. Williams, I'll explain everything to you in time, but I would really like to see Domenique first if you don't mind," Zack told them. He turned and started to walk toward one of the hospital rooms.

"Zack," I heard Mr. Williams say. "I have no idea who you are, but somehow I trust you."

Zack just turned around and very calmly said, "Everything is going to be okay. You have nothing to worry about." I saw smiles come to both Mr. and Mrs. Williams' faces.

47

Mrs. Williams walked up to Zack and put her hand on his chest. "I don't know how I know this, but I know you're here for a good reason." He smiled at her, grabbed her hand that was still on his chest, and gently gave it a squeeze. I just stood there, not really sure what I had just seen.

Zack looked over at me and asked, "What are you waiting, for Michael?"

I followed Zack into the hospital room. The room was about thirty feet long and there were three beds in it. Zack walked past the first bed in which a little boy rested. He looked to be about six or seven years old, and he was also an AIDS patient. Domenique was in the second bed and when she saw Zack, she lit up like a Christmas tree.

"Zack!" she screamed, her arms outstretched to invite a hug. Zack walked over to her bed and sat down on it, taking her in his arms. "I knew you would come," she told him. "I told my Mommy and Daddy you were coming, but I don't think they believed me."

"I'm here, Domenique" Zack told her. "Domenique, this is my friend Michael." Domenique looked at me and smiled. "Nice to meet you, Michael," she said, the smile never leaving her face.

"It is so very nice to meet you too, Domenique" I replied. I sat there and watched the two of them together for almost an hour, talking like they had known each other for years. Domenique told Zack about her parents, her dog, and the other children in the AIDS ward. Zack seemed to be a different person around her. I saw a kind and gentle side to him, one that I had not seen until now.

I heard the sound of footsteps behind me and looked back to see Domenique's parents and her doctor coming toward me. "Look Mommy, Daddy. He's here, just like I said he would be."

"Yes, sweetheart, I see him," Mrs. Williams told her. I could see that see was trying to hold back her tears. "Honey, you really need to get some rest. Maybe your friend Zack could come back to see you a little later." Mrs.

Williams put her hand on Zack's shoulder. I think she made the gesture to somehow assure her daughter that Zack would be here when she woke up.

"Zack, will you come back and see me later?" Domenique asked him.

"Of course I will. Don't you worry, I'll be here," Zack told her and then he bent over and kissed her on her forehead. "You get some rest, princess. I'll see you later." I watched both her parents kiss her cheek before all four of us walked out of the room, leaving only the doctor at her bedside. As touching as the scene was, I have to admit I was wondering what we were doing here.

Zack looked over at me and motioned for me to follow him. I walked with him down the hallway and we stopped at each door. In each room was a child who had somehow or other contracted the AIDS virus. Zack stepped into every room and stared at each child. I was not sure what he was doing, but he seemed to have some purpose. When we were finished going through the rooms, Zack turned around and walked back over to the Williams family. "Domenique is going to be fine. She's going to live," he told them. "In fact, all of these children are going to live." I was taken back by his words, but the Williamses just smiled at him, as if they somehow knew he meant what he'd said.

We left the hospital and Zack didn't speak a word to me. I decided it was wise to not try to initiate a conversation or ask him what he meant by the statement he had made in the hospital. We checked in at the Atlanta Marriot, and once we got up to the suite, Zack walked into one of the bedrooms and closed the door behind him. He had yet to utter a sound.

I went down to the lobby and ate dinner. When I returned to the room, Zack wasn't there. I had no idea where he had gone, but I was awakened at six o'clock the next morning to the sound of his voice.

"Get up, Michael, we have work to do."

Truth be told, I am not really a morning person. I prefer to wake up slowly, have a nice relaxing cup of coffee or two, and get my thoughts together. I guess today was not going to start the way I liked. "Okay Zack, what's the rush? Where are we going in such a hurry?"

"We are going to the CDC, Michael. I've got a disease to cure," Zack answered, and there was no sense of joking in his voice. Alright, I thought to myself, we are going to go to the Center for Disease Control—to do what? I was about to find out.

I got myself together as quickly as I could. We were out in front of the hotel in less than forty-five minutes, which meant it was still not even 8:00 a.m. There were a few cabs waiting out in front of the hotel and Zack motioned for one of them. The Marriot was only a few minutes from the CDC, and we were there before I could even finish the free cup of coffee I had poured in the hotel lobby.

"Okay, Zack, what exactly are we doing here? I haven't been to the CDC before, but I have a feeling they're not going to just let us walk freely through the building." A cocked smile formed on Zack's face as I spoke, and he did not answer me.

When we were about ten feet from the main entrance, he stopped suddenly and reached out his left arm like he was a crossing guard. "This is where it all starts, Michael. You've asked yourself why you are here. Well, today you will begin to know why."

I still did not have a clue what he meant, but, like Zack said, I was about to find out.

I walked up to the main doors and tried to open them, but they were locked. It appeared that the building had not yet opened. I looked back at Zack, who hadn't moved since he stopped, and once again he had that smile on his face. I heard a noise behind me, and when I turned around all the doors had been opened. Zack walked past me and looked back. "Come on, Michael, you don't want to miss this." *Miss what?* I thought to myself. I had come this far and I was not going to leave until I got some answers.

Besides, I have always been very curious and my curiosity was certainly piqued.

I followed Zack into the building, and I saw three security guards walking toward us. They were all armed. I was not sure what they were planning to do, but it didn't appear that they were there to welcome us. "The building is closed," said one of the guards, a pretty decent-sized man who had his hand on the gun he wore. I looked at the other two guards and they had taken the same posture, seemingly ready to draw their weapons should we say or do anything threatening. I decided the smartest thing for me to do was to just stand still. Zack, on the other hand, had a different approach and he walked toward the guards.

"I need you to take me immediately to where they do the research on AIDS. I also need you to gather anyone with any knowledge of AIDS research and bring them to me at the research area. Do you understand?" Zack asked.

To my disbelief, the guards replied, "Yes, sir, follow me, sir," and we were led to an elevator that required a key to open it.

I was still not sure exactly what just happened, and I was still not certain what we were going to accomplish here. It didn't take long before I found out. When the elevator doors opened, Zack motioned for me to follow him. One of the guards had left the elevator with us while the other two remained inside. Zack turned back to the two guards in the elevator. "Remember, anyone with any knowledge of AIDS research is to be brought to me." The two guards nodded their heads as the elevator doors closed.

I was not sure what to expect, but as we were led down the hallway, there were what appeared to be research laboratories. I could see a variety of equipment through the clear glass windows. In some ways it reminded me of my chemistry classes from years ago. We were led into a large room that, from the look of it, was some type of lab. The room was filled with computers and other types of equipment that I imagined were used for research.

I could see the other two guards coming down the hallway with a group of over a dozen men and women.

"What's going on here, and what are you two doing in my lab?" asked the first man that walked in the door. He looked to be in his fifties, with graying hair, not much of a sense of style, and it looked like he slept in his clothes.

"And you are—" Zack replied.

"I am Dr. Richard Hale. I head this team, and I want an explanation right now." By now, the remainder of the group was inside the room. Zack nodded to the three guards and they seemed to understand him. They left the lab and closed the door behind them. "Well, Dr. Richard Hale, my name is Zack Breeze, and this is Michael Ryan. Michael is a writer, and, me, well I am here to help."

"Help with what?" Dr. Hale asked.

"We are going to find the cure for AIDS, Doctor, and we are going to do it before lunch," Zack told them. Everyone in the lab must have thought Zack was joking. They all had smiles on their faces, and a few of them even laughed a bit. "Is all the information you have on AIDS in these computers?" Zack asked, pointing at the terminals scattered throughout the lab. He seemed unaffected by their disbelief or the fact they found his previous statement amusing.

"Part of our research is on these computers, yes, but they are linked to the mainframe which houses all of the information that has ever been gathered about the disease," Dr. Hale answered. His tone had changed from an angry to an inquisitive one. "Are you a researcher, a doctor, Mr. Breeze?" Dr. Hale asked.

"Like I said before, Dr. Hale, I am here to help. Now, let's get started," Zack sternly told him.

Zack walked over to one of the computer terminals and put his hands on it. Suddenly, the room began to fill up with documents from the computer—it looked as if the information were written in the air. Judging by the astonished looks on the faces of everyone in the room, no one had ever seen anything like this before. I sure as hell hadn't. Zack was standing in the center of the room. He appeared to be reading, though, incredibly fast, each document as it went by him. Zack walked back over to the computer once again. This time, he left his hands on the computer for about two minutes. I was not sure of this, but he seemed to be transferring all the information from the computer into his own mind. Once he was finished, he was back in the middle of the room, moving around the documents that were floating throughout the room, lining up some of them, and making others disappear.

"Dr. Hale!" Zack called out. The doctor, like everyone else in the room, was still mesmerized by what was going on. Zack had to call out to him three times before he answered.

"Yes, Mr. Breeze."

"You seemed to be on the right track here," Zack said as the pages of information he was referring to formed a circle around the group.

"We had some issues with stability," Dr. Hale replied.

"Okay, I can fix that problem, and I can also increase the potency of the drug ten thousand-fold," Zack told them. "Let's do this, people!" Zack yelled out like he was the quarterback in a big game. For starters, do you have any music in here?" Zack barked.

"We did have a boombox, but it broke last year," one of the researchers replied. Zack smiled and suddenly the music of the Grateful Dead filled the room. I sat there and watched in astonishment as they worked. Zack instructed everyone as he went from one work station to another. The information floating above kept changing with every step they took. Zack would occasionally play air guitar and dance around the room when the music moved him.

Outside the lab, a crowd had gathered. I wasn't sure if they were aware of what was going on or if they were just being curious. It was now almost 11:30 a.m. They had been working for less than three hours when I started hearing words like *amazing*, *impossible*, and *remarkable*. I walked over to where they were all huddled to see what they were talking about. "So, how's it coming?" I asked Zack.

"Your friend just discovered the cure for AIDS," Dr. Hale answered. My first thought was to reply with some cocky, sarcastic remark, but as I looked around at the group, it became obvious that they were not kidding. Somehow, in less than three hours, Zack had found a cure a disease that has killed millions of people.

They were all shaking hands and hugging, and then the doors to the lab opened. The crowd that had been watching from the hallway came in, and they cheered and hugged. It was quite a thing to see, but I had my eye on something else—Zack. I began to think back to what had prompted me to find him in the first place. All of the amazing, unbelievable stories I had been told now seemed not only believable, but likely. I had just watched this man cure a fatal disease in less time than it takes to cook a Thanksgiving turkey. Yes, just like everyone else in the room, I was happy. How could I not be having known people whose lives had been cut short by this horrible disease. But somehow, besides being just a bit nervous, I was very curious to know more about this man.

When everyone finally calmed down, Dr. Hale asked for everyone's attention. He wanted to say a few words. "Today is a day that many people will remember. I know I shall never forget what has happened here this morning. I have spent the last fifteen years of my life trying to find a way to cure this awful disease that has claimed the lives of so many millions of people."

"Mr. Breeze, I don't know who you are, or where you came from, or how you even got in here—and I do not care. I am sure many other people will offer you their thanks over the years, but allow me to be the first."

I suppose most people would have had some reaction to Dr. Hale's statement, maybe they would even have been humbled, but Zack seemed to take this all in stride with almost no emotion at all. He said thank you to everyone, and said he could not have done this without the help of Dr. Hale and his team, but I think everyone knew that was a lie. Anyone who watched what had transpired over the previous three hours would have realized that Zack was like a teacher, and they were all just doing as they were told.

Since Dr. Hale was in such a talkative mood, I decided to go ask him a few questions. I wanted to really understand the complexity of what Zack had done. I was more interested in how Zack helped them find the cure than in the cure itself. It wasn't easy, but I was able to get Dr. Hale away from the crowd and over to one of the corners of the lab. "Dr. Hale, as Zack told you, I'm a writer. I would like to know exactly how you were able to find the cure."

"Listen, Murray, I am not sure you really understand what your friend just did. He did not just find a cure for the disease, he destroyed it. I have never seen anything like this. You do understand what I'm saying, right?" With both hands, he pointed his fingers at me, trying to make sure what he said sunk in. I decided not to correct his calling me Murray, and I still was not sure what he was talking about.

"Doctor, I'm a writer. I was never much of a science whiz, so could you please explain to me exactly what you mean?"

"Alright, Murray, let me see if I can make you understand."

"Let's take polio as an example. Dr. Salk first tested his vaccine in 1952, and by 1980, at least in the U.S., polio was essentially eradicated. It was accomplished by making sure no one could get the disease. Do you follow me, Murray?" I nodded my head letting him know it was okay to continue.

"Now, you could say that Dr. Salk cured polio, some do, or you could say that Dr. Salk's vaccine just made those who received it immune to polio."

"So, Dr. Hale, are you saying that Zack has created a vaccine like Dr. Salk's?" I was still not sure I was following Dr. Hale's train of thought. He shook his head, obviously frustrated that I did not comprehend what he was trying to explain to me.

"Alright, let's try this, Murray. Your heart is failing, you need a transplant, but instead of an operation, imagine there is an injection you can get. Just one shot makes your heart work fine again. What your friend created is just like that, though in this case the disease is totally eradicated from the body."

"You mean that just one injection of what Zack created will cure someone who already has AIDS as well as prevent the disease in those who don't have it?"

"Now you're getting it, Murray."

Dr. Hale smiled as he began to walk back to the group. "Doctor, is that possible?" I yelled to him.

Dr. Hale turned around to look at me and yelled back, "It's not, at least not by any medical science we know of."

It seemed that the only people who were not cheering and hugging each other were Zack and me. Me, because this whole experience had me wondering even more—who exactly was this man? Zack, well, I'm not exactly sure why he showed no emotion one way or another.

I noticed Zack over in the corner of the lab working on something. I walked over to where he was sitting and watched as he poured a liquid into an array of test tubes, or at least that's what they looked like to me. "I guess I should be saying congratulations to you. Are you planning to go into another lab and cure cancer next?" I asked him jokingly.

"I am afraid that will have to wait until our next trip here, Michael," Zack answered. By the look on his face and the tone of his voice, he was totally serious. "We need to get back to the hospital. I made a promise to a little girl that I don't intend to break."

I noticed there were ten test tubes in the rack in front of him. He picked up the tray and handed it to me. "Michael, do me a favor and carry this."

"Sure," I answered. I took the tray from Zack and followed him as he made his way through the crowded lab.

Zack stopped when he reached Dr. Hale and his team. "Doctor, I want to thank you and your group for your help," Zack told him, reaching out his hand.

"Mr. Breeze, as much as I'd like to say we did something to help, we both know that you could have done this without any of us. I don't know who you are, but you have done the world a great service. I will be certain that everyone knows what you accomplished here today."

"Thank you, Doctor, but I didn't do this for recognition or for anyone's gratitude. As far as people knowing, that's what Michael is here for—to tell a story. What happened here today is just a part of that story."

I could tell by the look on Dr. Hale's face that he was not really sure what to make of Zack's little speech. As we made our way out of the lab, people were patting Zack on the back. I could tell that even though he was doing his best to be cordial, he had done what he came here to do, and he was eager to leave. We made our way to the elevator and back to the lobby. As we were approaching the front door, I could hear a female voice calling out to us.

Zack stopped and turned around. The look of annoyance on his face made me believe he knew who this woman was. He seemed to know what she wanted even before she started to speak. She looked to be in her late forties, though I had the feeling she was older. She was tall, almost model thin, and by the look of her arms she was in very good physical shape. "Gentlemen, my name is Dr. Eliza Walker. I am the head of the CDC. I heard about what you did here this morning. It appears there is no one in this building who hasn't heard about what you did." She looked over at me, her eyes fixed on the test tubes I was holding. "I understand neither of you are physicians or, for that matter, medical researchers." She continued talking at—not really to—us, and I could tell Zack was growing impatient.

"Yes, Dr. Walker, you are correct. Now, if you are finished, we have a little girl's life to save." I had seen that look on Zack before, and the last time I saw it someone got hurt. I was hoping that was not going to happen this time.

"I am sorry, gentlemen, but you must understand there are rules and protocols that exist when it comes to any new drug. There must be trials done before any new drug can be administered to the public."

Zack's face began to redden and his stare focused squarely on the doctor and the four security guards who had walked over, and were now standing behind her. "How many people have AIDS, Doctor?" There was now a noticeable anger in Zack's voice. "At least thirty or forty million." Zack was answering his own questions. "And how many die every day, how many, Doctor? And how many of those who die every day are children? Come on, Doctor, how many?"

"I understand your frustrations, but you must understand, I cannot allow you to take that medication out of here and begin to administer it to the public."

Well, that was the last straw, so to speak. Suddenly, the four guards collapsed to the floor, I wasn't sure if they were dead or just unconscious. The doors of the building blew off their hinges and fell to the ground. Zack reached out his arm and grabbed Dr. Walker by the throat, lifting her off the ground. Still clutching her, he walked over to a wall and pressed her against it, never letting her feet touch the ground.

"I have tried to be patient with you, you ignorant piece of flesh. I find you a cure for a disease that kills millions each year, and you quote rules to me. Perhaps you would not feel so noble if I gave this disease to you and everyone you care about. Maybe then, like all the others, you'd beg or pray for a cure. You listen to what I'm about to say, and you make sure every fucking word sinks into that pea-brain of yours. I am going to take this cure and save nineteen children. Once they are cured, it will be on the television news, in the newspapers, magazines, and on the internet. Everyone will know there is a cure, and everyone is going to want it. And guess what? You are going to make sure they get it. And if you or any of your bureaucratic pieces-of-garbage get in the way of that happening, I promise you, there is no power on earth that will protect you from what I will do to you. Do you understand me?" Zack stared into her eyes as he spoke to her. Her body at first tensed up, and then it started to shake. When he finally let go of her throat, she slumped down to the floor seemingly unable to move. Zack looked down at her and spoke to her again, this time not in anger but in an almost kind tone of voice. "You'll be alright in a few minutes and the guards will be as well. I'll be back soon to cure the rest of your diseases."

Zack turned and started walking toward the front doors again. "Come on, Michael, we have things to do." I followed Zack out of the openings in the building where the doors used to be. After we were outside, I heard a noise behind us. When I looked back, I saw the doors were back on their hinges just where they were before.

Zack hailed a cab and we were on our way to the hospital. I guess the shock of what I had witnessed in the last few hours had worn off, because suddenly my brain was trying to make sense of it all. This man, in a few hours, had cured one of the worst diseases known to man. From computers, he made images appear in the air. He was able to both control and disable someone with his mind. He somehow made the doors of a building fly off, and then he was able to put them back without ever lifting a finger. He seemed to either act in great kindness or great anger, and he seemed as eager to help as he did to hurt, depending on the situation. Well, I thought, not so different from most people I had met.

It was almost 1:00 p.m. by the time we arrived at the hospital. Mr. and Mrs. Williams were standing at the nurses' station as if they knew we were coming—something else I added to my mental notes of strange-but-true events. I did not realize at the time just how long that list was going to end up being.

"You did it," Melody Williams said as she first looked first at the tray of test tubes I was carrying, and then at Zack.

"Yes, I told you Domenique was going to live, and with just one injection she will be cured. I will not, of course, do anything without your permission. This is up to you. I will honor whatever decision you make."

The Williamses looked at each other for a moment. A strange smile came over both their faces. Then they turned back to look at Zack and me. "This will cure her?" James Williams asked Zack.

"Yes, James, this will cure her and every child in here, and everyone in the world who has AIDS."

"Then do it, please save our baby," Melody Williams pleaded to Zack, tears welling up in her eyes.

"Okay, Michael, here is what I need you to do. I want you to get the phone numbers of the parents of every AIDS-diagnosed child on this floor, and get them to come here as soon as they can." I looked over at Zack, and I guess he knew what I was going to say because before I had a chance to speak, he answered my question. "You didn't think I was going to inject these kids without their parents' permission, did you?"

"Alright, Zack, I'll go ask the nurses for the phone numbers."

Melody grabbed my arm. "No need to do that. I have everyone's contact information. We have something of a support group, and we call each other quite a bit.

"Thanks, Melody, I'll start calling them. Hey, Zack, exactly what should I tell them?"

"Tell them to get their asses down here, we would really like to cure their children, but we need them here first, or something like that."

I laughed to myself, thinking I'd come up with something just a bit more appropriate. I guess someone at the hospital found out why we were here because there was a small group coming down the hallway heading right for Zack and the Williamses.

"Dr. Price, this is the man I told you about. He has a cure for our baby," Melody Williams called out to one of the men walking toward them. The group consisted of four people: a woman and two men all wearing physicians' clothing, and a third man wearing a business suit. When they had reached Zack and the Williams couple, Dr. Price was the first to speak.

"Mrs. Williams, I know how much you want Domenique to get well, but do you honestly believe that this man could find a cure for her disease in just a few hours?" Dr. Price looked over at Zack and this time his words were directed at him. "Who are you? Are you telling these people that what is in those tubes is going to cure their daughter? How can you do this, give these people false hopes? You should be ashamed of yourself."

Zack smiled. I think he found the doctor's words somewhat amusing, and that's probably why the doctor was still standing.

"Excuse me," the man in the suit spoke up. "My name is James Radcliff and I am the hospital administrator. I'm sorry, but I cannot allow you to dispense that drug in this hospital. We cannot be involved or take responsibility for any such actions. I'm sure you can understand, Mr. and Mrs. Williams. We have to abide by the rules and we have our own liability issues to consider."

Okay, those were the last words from that group that Zack was going to listen to. His face contorted and the three doctors and the hospital administrator were suddenly airborne and stuck to the wall in the hallway. It was just like the kid's game where you throw Velcro balls against felt and they stick to it. They were trying to speak, their mouths were moving, but nothing came out. Zack walked over to them. "As you have probably figured out, you cannot speak, nor can you move," Zack told them. "I'm not going to hurt you, but I have heard all I want to hear today about what *cannot* be. I'm about to show you what *can* be, so pay very close attention. You are about to witness something great."

Zack turned and walked back toward the Williamses and they began to walk toward Domenique's room. I looked at the paper that Melody had given me. There were eighteen names on it and each name had at least two or three phone numbers next to it. I was trying to figure out exactly what to say to the parents. I didn't want to scare them, and I guess even after everything I had witnessed and everything I'd heard since I started this quest, I still did have my doubts that Zack had really cured AIDS.

I decided to tell the parents that something was happening right now at the hospital, and that it could change their child's condition. Yes, I was being vague, and they asked how, in what way, but I offered no answers. Instead, I told them they needed to come in person to have all the details explained. It took about thirty minutes to contact all the parents, and I was able to convince all of them to come to the hospital.

When I finished, I decided to go see what was happening in Domenique's room. I walked past the "wall art" and saw that the doctors and the administrator were still stuck. I wondered how Zack kept them from being injured when they hit that wall with so much force, they were stuck to it. I made another mental note about that one.

I walked into Domenique's room. She was smiling. This was certainly not the same little girl I had met yesterday. She started jumping up and down on the hospital bed. Next thing you know, she started to skip around the room. I'm no doctor, but all you had to do was look at her and you could tell she was better.

"Did you reach all the parents?" Zack asked me as I approached.

"Yes, they're all on their way. Is she——?"

"Cured? Yes, Michael, she is, and the damage to her body has been repaired." Domenique skipped over and stood in front of me, grabbed both of my hands, and jumped up and down. She let go after a couple minutes and went back to jumping up and down on the bed. Zack picked her up and gently put her down on the floor. "Remember, Domenique, I told you the doctors are going to want to examine you."

"Okay, Zack," she answered as he walked her out of the room. Her parents followed and Melody stopped and hugged me. "I want to thank you for bringing him to us," she whispered into my ear, and then she kissed my cheek. I am not sure why Melody thought I had anything to do with Zack's being here, but I wasn't about to say anything. She was enjoying the moment far too much for me to change the mood.

Zack walked Domenique out to the "wall hangings." Domenique laughed when she saw people stuck to the wall like that, and the strange thing was that her parents didn't even make a comment about it. Zack released them and gave them a warning before he restored their ability to speak. "Go do your tests. You will find there is no trace of the disease in her body."

Dr. Price walked over to Domenique and began to examine her. It was obvious by his expression that he was shocked. I think it was pretty clear to him just from a visual examination that something was different. "How can you be certain the disease is gone?" he asked Zack. "Well, Doctor, do as many tests as you like. You will find nothing wrong with this little girl," Zack answered.

"Did I just hear you say Domenique is cured?" a voice from behind me said. We all turned around. There was a group of what I'm sure were the parents of the other infected children standing there.

"Yes, Domenique is cured," Zack told them. "And I can cure all of your children as well. All I need is your permission to give them an injection." They all looked at Domenique who was jumping, running, skipping, and looking like she was in perfect health, and then they looked at Zack.

"How can this be?" asked one of the parents. "We were all told there was no cure, no real hope for our kids to survive this disease."

"This man is our hope," Melody Williams spoke out. "Look at Domenique. She's fine now." Zack looked at all of the parents. By the size of the group that had gathered around us, it looked like most or all of the parents had arrived. Zack looked over at me, nodded his head, and smiled. I think it was his way of saying job well done. All you could hear was the sound of chatter as the parents talked among themselves. Meanwhile, Domenique was running up and down the hallway.

Zack raised his hands up over his head in an attempt to get them all to stop talking. It did not seem to be working and finally he yelled out. "Would you all please be quiet and listen!" Finally, it was quiet. "My name is Zackary Breeze. This morning this man and I went to the CDC. With the help of the AIDS research team, we were able to come up with a medicine that I injected into Domenique less than one hour ago. The CDC knows that this will cure the disease. It will cure all of your children. However, as I am sure the doctors standing here will verify, they will not allow the cure to be used until it is studied and scrutinized. There will need to be what they call human trials. All of this will take years. In the meantime, your children and many others may die while the cure is right here." Zack lifted the medicine up over his head. "I will ask all of you the same question I asked James and Melody: Do you want your child to live? If the answer is yes, then go stand by the door of your child's room and I will give them the medicine."

They all looked at each other, then at Zack, but mostly they watched Domenique as she happily skipped around us singing. The group began to separate, each of them standing by the doors of one room or another.

Zack seemed pleased with their decisions. He looked over at the doctors and spoke to them. "I was kind to you earlier, but if you get in my way again, I will make sure you suffer more than any one of these children has. Do you understand me?" Dr. Price put his hands up as if to acknowledge surrender, and then nodded his head. The other three followed his lead and made the same gestures. "How long will it take you to get the results of Domenique's blood test?" Zachary asked him.

"If we put a rush on it, about two hours," Dr. Price answered.

"Well, put a rush on it. I want there to be medical proof when the announcement is made," Zack told them, and then he walked over to me. "Michael, you did so well getting all the parents here. I need to ask another favor."

"What would you like me to do for you this time, Zack?"

"I need you to call all of the local television stations and newspapers and get them down here at four today."

"Alright, Zack, I hope you know what you're doing. You know, that Dr. Walker at the CDC was right about what she said. They are not going to release this drug to the world without doing some sort of testing."

"You let me worry about that, Michael. You just get them down here."

"Alright, but don't say I didn't warn you." Zack just smiled and walked away, heading for the first room. The two sets of parents waiting there for him smiled and followed him into the room.

I guess you could say I was still not a believer. I did as Zack asked, but I did not use my own name when I made the calls. I told them to consider me an unnamed hospital source. Even though I knew what my eyes had seen, I just could not make myself believe that all of it was true. Maybe because if it was all really true, it meant I had to start to consider that the man I was traveling with was something other than—damn, I was not remotely ready to go there. Get it together, Michael, I thought to myself.

After I finished making the phone calls, I decided I had better give Julie a call. I wanted to fill her in on what had happened over the last two days. I headed down to the lobby and walked out of the hospital, looking for a quiet place where my conversation would not be heard.

Julie answered the phone after several rings.

"So what happened with the little girl? Did your mystery man cure her?"

"Julie, we went to the CDC this morning. He discovered a cure for AIDS in less than three hours."

"What? You're sure? That seems completely impossible to me."

"Well, I was there, and trust me, it still seems completely impossible to me, too."

I filled Julie in on the rest of the things that happened, though I did leave out a few details like Zack turning four people into "wall art." I figured this story was hard enough to believe without adding that part to it. "Well," Julie said, "I guess your instincts were right. It looks like this is going to be quite a story. I assume you're going to stick with it," she laughed.

"Yes, I am. I have a feeling there's something even bigger than what's already happened. I just don't know exactly what it is yet," I told her.

"Okay, but remember what I said before. You're not the hero type, Michael, you're the watch-someone-else-be-the-hero type, and then write-about-the-hero type of guy."

I laughed, "Yeah, you are so right about that one." Don't worry, I have no plans of changing that anytime soon."

We said our goodbyes and I ended the call. Maybe I should have told her I missed her or something to that effect, but the truth was that I was so caught up in what was going on that I hadn't really had the time to think about anything else. I started to run a few things through my mind, and each time I did, I either didn't like the explanation I came up with, or it was just too bizarre to believe. I would think, *who is Zack?* Then I would think, *what is Zack?* He has avoided answering any of the real questions I'd asked him, and the ones he did answer, I began to think were not answered truthfully. Even though I was pretty sure of the outcome, I gave my researchers a call and asked them to find out anything they could about the Breeze family from Bala Cynwyd, Pennsylvania. If my intuition was correct, there would be no such family.

By the time I returned to the AIDS ward, all of the children had been given the medication. The floor had been transformed from a gloomy, silent place to a playground for active, happy kids. A part of me wanted to call the researchers and tell them, never mind, if he can do this, does it really matter who he really is? But the journalist in me said that a story cannot be written without all the facts.

The journalist in me won. I walked over to Zack. He was being hugged and thanked by all of the parents. "Nice job," I said to him, and reached out to shake his hand. He grabbed my hand, pulled me in, and gave me a hug.

"Yes, Michael, this is just the first lesson," he whispered in my ear. He smiled and let me go. I didn't know what he meant, but I figured I'd find out soon enough. Dr. Price and about twenty others dressed like doctors were heading toward us. Dr. Price had some papers in his hands and was waving them at Zack. He walked up to Zack and handed him the papers.

"Do you know what these results mean?" Dr. Price asked him.

Zack looked down at the papers, and then back at Dr. Price. "Yes, I do," Zack answered. "Please tell Melody and James what your tests results are." There was a sudden silence as all of the parents were waiting to know what they had found.

"There is absolutely no trace of the disease in Domenique's body. In fact, it appears that there was never any disease there at all. There is nothing that can scientifically account for this, but Domenique is a hundred percent cured."

I looked around and saw many of the parents begin to cry. "Thank you," Dr. Price said. Zack reached out to shake the doctor's hand as he spoke to him. "I'm sorry I had to restrain you earlier, but as you can see, this needed to be done." I was a little shocked to hear Zack apologize. The man I had been observing up to this point did not strike me as the type who was used to saying he was sorry.

"I'm told your name is Zack Breeze," Dr. Price spoke tentatively to Zack.

"Yes, you can just call me Zack."

"Zack, how did you do this?"

"Just a lot of luck, Doctor, and just a little help from my friends." Zack smiled.

"Okay, Doctor, let me tell you what is going to happen next. In an hour or so, there are going to be television and newspaper reporters here to report what has happened today You see that man?" Zack pointed over to me. "He's a writer. You are going to read a statement he has written for you."

"You want me to tell the world about this? Perhaps I'm not the right person. You might want someone of greater stature to make this type of announcement."

"No, Doctor, you will do just fine, and I'm sure all of these good people here will be glad to stand next to you while you do it." There was a collective yell of *yes* from the parents, and Zack got his way.

He looked over at me, and I just shook my head. I had never written a press release before, but it would be my pleasure to write this one. Zack walked over to me and motioned for me to follow him. We entered one of the empty hospital rooms and he closed the door behind us. "I don't want you to mention my name in your little speech."

"Why? I watched you, Zack. You can say whatever you like to everyone else, but I was there, remember? You created this cure."

"Yes, I did, Michael, but for now you are not to mention my name. We have much more to do, Michael, and it will be easier to accomplish if you do not mention my name yet." As usual, I didn't know what he meant, but what the hell, I did as he asked.

I wrote the press release. Zack and I waited until about five minutes to four before we headed down to the lobby. I was pretty surprised when I saw how many people had shown up, including some I did not contact. There were about thirty-five people there from the various media outlets, and probably another fifty people who were just curious to know what was going on.

Dr. Price approached the microphones. He was surrounded by the children, their families, and hospital staff members. "I have a brief statement to read." The doctor cleared his throat before going on. "Today is a monumental day in the world of medical science, for today is the day that we no longer have to lose any more lives to the disease commonly known as AIDS. While there were many people involved in finding the means to eradicate this disease, the children and their families who are standing up here with me would like to especially thank Dr. Richard Hale and his team from the CDC for their special contribution. The children standing next to me were all inflicted with the AIDS virus, and they all stand here today—completely cured."

Once Dr. Price finished his statement, the questions came from everywhere. They were directed not only at him, but to the hospital administrator, and Domenique as well.

Dr. Price tried his best to be vague and still offer some kind of an answer, but he was ill-prepared for the barrage of questions thrown out at him. I felt sorry for the man because he began to look almost foolish up there. Finally, the hospital administrator stepped in and ended the briefing. He thanked everyone for coming, and said there would be more information released in the coming days. I doubt he had a clue as to what that information might be, but it did sound good, and it worked. The reporters realized they were not getting anything further today. I looked over at Zack, and he seemed amused by what he had just witnessed. "Maybe we should have prepared him better," I said to him.

"Oh, he's fine, Michael. All I wanted was for the world to know that the cure exists. Let's see what the world does with it now." I wanted to continue this conversation, but Domenique ran over and jumped onto Zack's lap, wrapping her arms around his neck. "Was that fun?" Zack asked her.

"I don't think Dr. Price knew how to answer those people's questions, but it was fun. Everyone took my picture," she said.

"How are you feeling, Domenique?" I asked her. "I'm feeling fine. I'm very hungry, though. Can we go get something to eat?'

Melody and James walked over to where we were sitting. Melody shook her index finger, waving it from side to side, smiling and looking right at Zack. "Shame on you, Zack Breeze. You let that poor man go in front of those reporters not knowing a damn thing about what he was talking about." She laughed and put her hand on Zack's shoulder. "But I will love you until the day I die," she told him as she bent over and kissed him on the cheek.

"I don't know how we can ever thank you enough or express how grateful we are to you," James said to him as he reached for his hand. Zack took his hand and he smiled, nodding his head. I would have thought Zack might have said something to the Williamses, like maybe *you're welcome*, or *no need to thank me*, but he said nothing.

I think the Williamses were waiting for his reply as well, so I decided to break the silence. "I'm hungry too, let's eat," I said. It seemed to work. We were now all headed for the cafeteria. We all walked into the dining area except for Zack. When I looked back, he was just standing in the doorway.

The Williamses had also noticed that Zack was not walking along with us, and we began to walk back toward him. "I am sorry, but Michael and I must leave now," he said. "Someone I used to know is in trouble, and we have to go and help her."

"You mean like the way I was in trouble before you came here?" Domenique asked him.

"Yes, something like that. Someone's been hurt and I have to go and help her. I promise I'll be back, and when I do, if it's okay with your parents, you can come with me to the place where they look for cures to diseases, and we'll help more people together."

Domenique smiled at him and outstretched her arms like she wanted Zack to pick her up. Zack picked her up, gave her a big hug, and then shook both her parents' hands. "What's your friend's name, Zack?" Melody asked as we started to walk away.

"Janice," Zack replied.

"We'll be praying for her!" Melody yelled back at us.

"What's going on?" I asked Zack as we left the hospital.

"We're going to San Francisco, Michael," was all he said when he answered me.

71

We stopped at the hotel, grabbed our bags, and checked out. Within minutes we were on a plane headed for San Francisco. I certainly didn't want to see a friend of Zack's in pain, but the thought of meeting someone who had known him for years did interest me a great deal.

Zack was not very talkative on the plane, which was fine with me. I was tired and I took the opportunity to take a nice long nap. The flight was uneventful and we landed on time. Since all we had were carry-on bags, we made our way quickly to the front entrance. When we got outside, the black Lexus SUV was parked right in front of the airport. We walked over to it and at first I thought, wow, he had somehow rented the same car as before. Then I looked inside and there were my other two bags and the wrapper from the nuts I had eaten. This *was* the same car, and it was here before we arrived, and it was parked in front of a major airport. Okay, so how did the car get here? And with all the security at airports these days, how could it just be parked in front of a major airport, with no one in it without be towed or impounded? I made another of my how-is-this-possible mental notes and climbed in the passenger side.

"So, exactly where are we going?" I asked.

"We are going to the University of California Medical Center." That was all Zack said and I had a feeling that was all he was going to say at the moment, so I just sat there and enjoyed the ride.

When we arrived at the hospital, Zack decided it was the right time to tell me why we were here. "There is a woman up in intensive care. She was once an important part of my life. She probably will not remember this, but I once told her I would always be there for her if she ever needed me. Well she needs me now, Michael. The doctors here are unable to do anything more for her. I am the only chance she has to survive."

"I'm sorry, Zack. We never really had the chance to talk about anyone who was important to you." We made our way through the hospital, heading for the intensive care unit. When we arrived, there were two large doors and a sign that read "No Admittance. Authorized Personnel Only." Well,

I didn't really think that was going to stop Zack and, of course, it didn't. The doors flung open, and I followed him through them. A nurse started walking toward us. Before she could even open her mouth, she dropped to the floor unconscious. We made our way down the hall, stopping at the fourth room.

I looked into the room, and there was no one in there. The next room had an empty cart in front of it, and I could hear voices that seemed to be coming from that room. "San Francisco police! Put your hands where I can see them and slowly turn around." The voice came from behind us. Zack and I raised our hands over our heads and slowly turned around to find a police officer standing there, his gun out of its holster and pointed right at us. He must have been there to guard Zack's friend, and I'm sure seeing the unconscious nurse made him doubt we were there to help anyone. He tried to use his radio, but it apparently was not working.

"We're here to help," Zack told him. "I will ask you only once to put your weapon away."

"You're in no position to ask anything, asshole," the officer replied. Well, those were the last words I would hear him speak. Suddenly, his gun left his hands. It moved so fast I could barely see it, and in an instant, it was in Zack's hand. He crushed it like a paper cup and dropped it on the ground. Zack reached out his arm and the police officer's feet left the ground, his body heading toward Zack. What stopped his movement was Zack's hand, now clamped around his neck. I could see the fear in his eyes.

"Zack, please," I started to speak, but was cut off.

"No need to worry, Michael, I'm not going to hurt him. I just need some answers." Zack held him like that for about a minute and then gently let him down to the ground. Like the nurse, he was unconscious. Answers, I thought, answers to what? Zack never asked him a thing.

I turned back toward the room, and the noise had brought a flurry of doctors and nurses out into the hallway. I also saw a group of people come around the corner and walking toward us. "Who are you, and what are you doing here?" one of the men demanded. I assumed by his clothing he was one of the attending physicians.

"His name is Zackary Breeze," I heard a voice say. I looked over toward the voice. The the words I heard were spoken by an elderly woman. If I had to guess, I would say she was in her late seventies to early eighties. She pushed her way through the crowd of doctors and nurses and stood in front of Zack.

"Hello, Gwen," Zack said as he hugged her.

She looked straight at him and said. "she needs you, Zack. They can't do anything more for her."

I glanced across the room and saw there was a woman in the bed. She must have been in her early fifties at least. She looked to have been badly beaten. She was hooked up to quite a few monitors, and she had an oxygen mask over her face. "Everything is going to be fine, Gwen," Zack told her as he began to walk into the room. One of the doctors began to protest, but Gwen put her hand on his chest and said, "you've already told us there is nothing you can do. He can save her and I ask you to let him." The doctor said nothing as Zack entered the room and closed the door. There were curtains covering all of the windows, so none of us was able to see what was going on inside the room.

Less than five minutes had gone by when Zack opened the door. There was a collective gasp as we all looked inside the room. The woman no longer had any marks on her body.

The tubes, the test lines, and even the oxygen mask had been removed. "She's resting. She should wake up in a couple hours," Zack told Gwen. He seemed to treat her with a certain reverence that I had not previously seen in him. "We have to leave now, Gwen. The man who did this needs to be stopped. Once that's done, I'll be back."

"You get that bastard, Zackary! You make him pay!" Gwen yelled out as we walked away.

"So tell me, Zack, what exactly is going on?" I asked as we headed out of the hospital.

"There is a man who has been kidnapping, torturing, and killing children. So far, he has murdered four, and the fifth would have been a seven-year-old boy. Janice saw the kidnap attempt and tried to help the child. The boy got away, but the killer took out his frustration on Janice in a fit of rage.

"My God! What kind of animal could do something like that?"

"You can ask him when we find him, Michael." Within a few minutes we were back on the road. I wasn't sure where we were headed, and I didn't ask. The more time I spent with Zack, the more unanswered questions I had. I have never been a believer in the unknown. I have always thought there was a logical explanation for everything that happened, but I didn't have a single rational explanation for anything that had occurred since I met Zack. I was fairly confident that whatever limited information he had given me was merely to satisfy my curiosity, and was likely not the truth. I also knew, like I had told Julie, that I was going to stick with Zack. There was something much bigger going on here, and I was going to find out what it was. I didn't know at that point that I was going to wish that I had never found out.

We weaved our way through the city traffic and as we pulled into a parking lot, I could see what our destination was. The sign on the building across from us read San Francisco Police. Zack parked the car and we made our way toward the building. I kept looking over at him as we walked. I guess he must have somehow known what was on my mind. "Stop worrying, Michael, I'm not going to hurt anyone in there. I just need to know what information they have about this piece-of-shit killer."

I'm not sure they're going to voluntarily give up that information, Zack."

"Well, Michael, I think they just might."

I thought to myself, this is going to be interesting.

We entered the building and, as I suspected, there was quite a crowd in the lobby. About thirty feet from the front door, there was what appeared to be a check-in desk with two uniformed officers. Zack headed right for the two officers, both already very busy dealing with the requests of the crowd that filled the lobby. As Zack walked up, they both stopped talking and looked over at him. "They're on the second floor, Room C." Zack nodded his head and motioned for me to follow him over to the elevator. We found the room which was identified by a piece of paper with *C* scrawled on it and taped to the fake wooden door. Inside there were about fifteen police officers, some in uniform and others in plain clothes. There was a large bulletin board on wheels that had several photos tacked on to it.

We walked up to the board and the photos were enough to turn my stomach. They were obviously the crime scene photos, and I hope none of you ever have to view anything like what I saw on that board. There was also a picture of Janice taken after the suspect had beaten her.

Zack removed Janice's photo from the board, turned around, and held the photo up to eye level. "This woman is a very special friend of mine," he yelled out to the room. "I want to find whoever did this. I need to know everything you have on him, and I need it now."

One of the officers began to approach us in an aggressive manner. Zack lifted his index finger and moved it from side to side, trying to send a not-a-good-idea message to him. The message did seem to be understood, though, and some of the other officers now had their hands on their weapons. Zack noticed it as well and in an instant all of them were pinned again the wall. "Okay, I can see you assholes are not going to let me do this the nice way. Who's in charge here? No answer? Alright, it seems it's going to take a bit more convincing to get you to cooperate."

I watched as two of the uniformed officer's guns were—I guess the best way to describe it—levitated out of their holsters and moved to the center of the room, suspended in mid-air. I saw the looks of shock and fear on the faces of the officers in the room. The two guns were then crumpled up, each into a small ball, and then they fell to the ground. "I could have just as easily done that to your heads," Zack yelled out. "I am going to ask you just one more time, who the fuck is in charge here?"

"I am." The answer came from a tall, balding man. "Lt. James Farros. And who are you?"

"Well for now, you can just think of me as a concerned citizen, and if that doesn't work for you, then you can think whatever you want. But regardless of what you think, you are going to give me every bit of information you have on the person who did these things."

"Janice Tauten—you say you know her?" the lieutenant asked. "Is she a family member?"

"Lieutenant, do not try my patience with your feeble attempt to get me to reveal things to you." You can either tell me where all your files are, or I can rip the information out of all your minds, and believe me, that will be an excruciatingly painful experience. Have I made myself clear?"

"Alright, alright, what you're looking for is in the cabinet on the right-side top drawer."

Zack walked over to the cabinet and removed a large stack of papers. He laid them out on the desk in front of him and, just as he had done at the CDC, made images of all the file material appear in the air all around the room. "Holy shit," I heard someone in the room say. Zack moved the images around the room. I think he was looking for a place to start. There were pictures of about forty men in the files. I imagined they were possible suspects, and Zack seemed most interested in them. "Which one of these pieces-of-shit looks the most promising?" Zack asked.

"Can I speak?" said a voice from the crowd of officers.

Zack turned and walked over to the man. "Who are you?" he asked.

"Detective Steve Reton. I caught the case after the first murder. I have been on this from the beginning," he answered.

"Alright, I'm going to let all of you down, but do not test me. I am only here to catch whoever did this. I won't hurt any of you unless you do something stupid. Do we understand each other?" The officers either nodded or spoke out *yes*, and Zack released them from the wall. "Now, Detective, tell me what you know."

I think everyone realized Zack wanted the same thing they did, because no one made a dash for the door or attempted to use the phone. Instead, they began to look at the images and spoke among themselves trying to come up with some possible new angle to the case. They went from trying to pull their guns on us to being more than willing to work with us, like we were now part of the team.

"At first we looked in the usual places, perps who had histories of sexual assaults, but no one in our system had an MO like this. Then we tried the FBI's database, but still nothing."

"So you think this guy has never murdered before?" Zack asked.

If he has, he's changed his tactics. The guy we want is a very violent sexual predator. What he did to those kids, well you have to be a pretty sick fuck to be able to do something like that to a child. There's one other lead that's not in our files."

"Really? Why is that?"

"Well, I really didn't like this guy as the doer, but there's something about him and what he does that makes me uneasy."

"Tell me more." Zack was interested.

"The guy's name is Bobby Macklin. He writes these weird adult comic books. Yeah, I know it's a stretch, but these comic books are graphic and very violent, and even children are victims in his comics."

"And," Reton said, "the guy has no real history of violence, in fact, outside a pot bust years ago, he's clean, and he has an airtight alibi for one of the murders."

"But you think he is connected to this in some way?" I asked him.

"Yes, I do," Reton replied, "but we have nothing to bring him in on. I did go to see him, but he wasn't exactly eager to answer my questions. I think you guys might have more luck at persuading him to talk."

"Thank you, Detective. Michael, I think we have all we need from here." We took copies of all the profiles of the suspects they had, along with a copy of Detective Reton's notes on Bobby Macklin. On the way out the door, Zack told them who we were, first names only. He grabbed one of their handheld radios and told them we would be in touch when we found the scumbag who did this. As we walked out of the station, I saw a copy of the *San Francisco Chronicle* on one of the desks. The front-page headline read: "A Cure For AIDS?" I would grab a copy later.

"I saw it, Michael, but we have more important things to do at the moment. Janice stopped him from taking that child, and he's going to want another one fast. We need to find him before he gets that chance."

"I assume we're going to start with Bobby Macklin?" I'm not sure why I asked. I knew that was where we were going. The detective's notes said Bobby owned an S&M store in the SOMA neighborhood. I didn't know what that meant, but Zack must have. He knew exactly where he was going, and we were soon parked off 8th Street. The sign on the building we entered said Bobby's Den. I must admit though I am not exactly a prude, this was the first time I had ever walked into any type of an adult store. I was amazed at some of the things that were sold in there. I picked up this collar with a ball on it, wondering what purpose this could possibly have. I put it down and joined Zack at the counter.

If I had to imagine who would work at a place like this, I probably would have pictured the woman who was behind the counter. She was wearing a black leather jump suit and black thigh-high boots. She had her fair share of piercings and tattoos, and her jet black hair had streaks of red and blue in it.

"Can I help you gentlemen with anything?" she asked us.

"I'm looking for Bobby," Zack answered her.

"Bobby!" she called out, turning her head to the doorway behind the counter. "There are two guys here to see you."

Bobby Macklin came through the doorway. He was probably in his early thirties and he looked like a heavy metal rocker with his long hair and his AC/DC T-shirt. He was over six feet tall and he must have been a heavy drinker, since I could smell the alcohol as soon as he walked through the door.

"What can I do for you guys?"

"I wanted to talk to you about these," Zack told him, holding up one of Bobby's comics.

"Oh, you're a fan! Cool," Bobby said.

"Do you have a lot of fans?" Zack asked.

Bobby's eyes moved from Zack to me. "Who are you guys? You don't look like cops."

"We aren't cops, Bobby," Zack told him. "All we want is your help. You see, we think that maybe the guy who's out there killing children might also be one of your fans, and we think you just might have some idea who he might be."

"I don't know what the fuck you're talking about, now get the fuck out of my store before I kick the crap out of both of you."

Well, that was not exactly the answer Zack was looking for. He grabbed Bobby by the front of his shirt and threw him right out the front window of the store.

Before leather-jumpsuit girl could even scream, she was on the ground, unconscious. It was about thirty-five feet from the counter to the front window. Zack threw him with such a force that he went right through it hitting the side of a car parked on the street, and putting a huge dent in the car. Bobby was lying on the ground, half-conscious, and bleeding from multiple parts of his body. Zack bent over and grabbed him by the throat, lifting him of the ground like he weighed nothing.

"Wake up, little Bobby," Zack said as if he were talking to a child.

"Zack, I don't think he even knows his name right now."

"Well, Bobby, Michael thinks you don't even know your name, but I can feel you waking up in there." Zack poked his finger into Bobby's forehead. "So listen to me very carefully, Bobby, you can either help me find the man who has killed those children, or you can bleed to death right here on this street. The choice is yours, Bobby, but make it fast. I'm not in the mood to be patient."

"Okay, but you have to get me to a hospital. I'm dying here."

"Tell me now, Bobby, or I'll kill you myself."

"The guy you're looking for hangs out near the children's playground in Golden Gate Park. He has long, reddish hair, always wears a fucking ugly, orange leather jacket with a basketball on the front left side, and a baseball cap. "I don't know his real name, but he calls himself Squid. That's all I know. Now get me to the fucking hospital."

Bobby passed out on the sidewalk. I looked behind me and saw that leather-girl was now outside the store, still unconscious. She was lying on the ground a few feet from the store entrance. I suddenly heard the sound of glass breaking as Bobby's store collapsed. In an instant, there was nothing there but dust. Zack used the radio he had taken to contact the police, and let them know where to send the ambulance. But that was all he told them. He didn't mention anything Bobby had told us or that we were headed for Golden Gate Park.

It took us about twenty-five minutes to make our way there. The playground was a marvel with structures and tubes for kids to climb in, and something I had not seen in years, a carousel. And not just any carousel. It was huge and ornate, like nothing I had ever seen before.

"You know, Michael, there used to be thousands of carousels in playgrounds all over this country, and now only a few hundred are left."

"I didn't know that, Zack. I haven't spent a lot of time in playgrounds." Zack grabbed my arm and pointed to a woman who was walking around the playground. She was clearly looking for someone. We walked toward her, and as we got closer we could hear her calling out, "Missy, Missy." Zack seemed to already know what was going on. He walked up to her and asked if everything was okay.

"I can't find my daughter," she told him with worry in her voice.

"What does she look like?" Zack asked her.

"She has blond hair, and she's wearing a pink shirt and carrying a Barbie doll," the woman answered.

"We'll help you find her," Zack said. "Michael, come with me."

"Zack, do you know something?" I asked.

"He took her, Michael. I can sense it." Zack motioned for me to follow him and we headed over to the parking lot. The woman was right behind us. When we got there, we saw the Barbie doll lying there on the ground. Zack put it in his back pocket.

"Oh my God!" The woman yelled out. "Did someone take her?"

"Don't worry," Zack told her. "I'm going to get her back for you."

We heard the screech of tires, and we looked in the direction the sound came from. We saw a beige van speeding out of the parking lot. "That's him," Zack told me. "Come with me, Michael, and bring her along." I turned around and touched the woman's arm.

"Come with us. I promise you, he will get your daughter back for you."

Zack ran toward the van as it weaved in and out of the traffic in the lot, trying to get to the exit. I heard a loud popping sound as all four of the van's tires were suddenly flattened. We were still a good distance away, but I could see the man in the orange jacket exit the van. He was holding the little girl in his right arm. He started to run across the parking lot. I could hear the little girl screaming for her mother. He made it out of the parking lot and across the street. He then ran down an alley between two buildings. Zack waited for us at the entrance of the alley.

"Michael, call this in on the radio. Tell them where we are." I let the police know where we were. I described the man and told them he was holding a little girl hostage. They told us to wait for them to arrive, but

Zack had no intention of doing that. "Michael, come with me. Miss, you wait right here. Everything is going to be fine."

I looked over at the mother and she seemed to be in a daze, just standing there as we walked down the alley. When we got to the end of the alley, there was Squid. He was holding the little girl in front of him. He had his left hand over her mouth, and in his right hand was some sort of knife.

"Stop right there," he yelled out. "I'll cut her throat if you come one step closer."

"You do not want to hurt that little girl," Zack told him. "It's over, Squid. Now let her go and maybe you might live past today."

"Fuck you, asshole!" Squid yelled out. "This little bitch dies today."

Suddenly, both of Squid's arms were raised over his head and he was catapulted off the ground, his feet slamming into the wall at the end of the alley. The little girl ran toward us.

"Take her to her mother, Michael," Zack told me as I scooped the girl into my arms. "Now, Michael!" his voice commanded.

I carried the little girl out of the alley, and her mother's face lit up as she saw me with her daughter safe in my arms. By that time, the police had arrived and they immediately began asking me questions.

"I need to get back there," I told them, but the officers restrained me from returning to Zack.

"Let him go," I heard a voice instruct. It was Detective Reton. He walked over to me.

"He found the perp?" asked Reton.

"Yes, Detective, now please let me go back down there."

"I afraid I can't do that."

"You're not sending any officers down there, are you? You're going to let Zack do what he wants to that man, aren't you?"

It was already too late to save Squid. I saw Zack walking toward us. "You can call for a body bag, Detective, but you might have to look around for all the pieces."

No one said a word to Zack as he walked past them, or made any attempt to stop him. We walked out of the alley together. The camera crews from the local television stations were already there, and there was an ambulance parked off to the side of the entrance to the alley.

Zack walked over to the ambulance and opened the back door. The little girl and her mother were inside. Zack pulled the Barbie doll from his back pocket and reached out to give it to the girl's mother. "I think this belongs to your daughter," he said to her.

"I don't know how I can ever thank you," the mother gushed to him as she gave him a hug. Zack reached over and touched the side of the little girl's face, and she smiled at him.

"She will never remember this day," Zack told her mother. "But you will. Teach her well."

Zack closed the door of the ambulance and we started to walk back toward where our car was parked. I wondered what he meant when he told the mother to teach her well. I was going to have to ask him about that at some point. As we walked by the news crews, they pointed the cameras at us. They were extending their microphones to ask us if it was true that we had caught the suspect. Zack paid no attention to the reporters, and once again I found myself trying to make sense out of what had happened.

I recounted the events of the last day in my mind. First off, the car we had left in a Georgia airport parking lot car was waiting for us when we arrived in San Francisco. Next, we went to see Zack's friend who lay dying in the hospital and with a mere touch of his hand, her wounds miraculously healed. And then, Zack coerced the cooperation of the police, caused a building to collapse, and he more than likely just killed a man while a crowd of police officers just let him walk away! I was having a really hard time coming up with a logical explanation for anything that happened in the last eighteen hours, and I think that is exactly the way Zack wanted me to see it.

We were back in the car and on the move again, though this time I had a pretty good idea of where we were going. My hunch proved right when I saw the hospital. When we got off the elevator and started to walk down the hallway, the televisions were all showing the breaking news report. Though I could not hear what was being said, they were showing the footage of Zack and me walking from the alley.

When we got to Janice's room, she was sitting up in her bed watching the report. Her mother and the other three people I had seen earlier were also in the room. It turns out they were Janice's husband, her twenty-two-year-old daughter, and her twenty-year-old son. Janice saw Zack and smiled, tears flowing down her face. She reached out her arms to him, and Zack walked over to the bed and hugged her.

"Thank you, Zack," she said, her voice shaking as she kept crying. "Look at you, you haven't changed a bit, and it's been twenty-five years."

"Good genes," Zack told her.

"Yeah, sure, and I'm the Queen of Sheba," Janice replied slapping Zack in the arm. Janice picked up the newspaper that was lying next to her on the bed. "You did this too, didn't you?" she said, pointing to the "AIDS Cured" headline. Zack didn't answer her, but she seemed to already know that the answer was yes. "I always knew you were different, I just never knew how different until now. Now, who is this man with you?"

"Janice, this is Michael Ryan. Michael is a writer and he's here to write a story."

"Well, Michael Ryan, it's nice to meet you," Janice said as she reached out her had toward me. I walked over and shook her hand. "So, may I ask what kind of a story you're working on?"

"I'm really not that sure at the moment. I don't quite yet have enough of the facts or information I need." Yes, I was being evasive, but at that point I really didn't have most of the facts.

"So how do you know Zack? You didn't tell him, did you?" Janice looked over at Zack as she spoke. "I guess I can understand why you didn't. You see, Michael, twenty-six years ago I met this pretty amazing guy. We had a great year together, and I really loved him. I would have married him if he had asked me, but instead one day he told me that he had to leave and that he was sorry. He offered no explanation. All he said was that was the way it had to be. I never forgot how he broke my heart, and until today I never forgave him for it." Janice smiled as she spoke those words. "If you all don't mind, I would like to talk to Zack alone for a moment."

We walked out into the hallway, though as we all stood there waiting no one spoke a word. It was as if no one knew what to say. We had all seen what Zack had done, and now to find out that Zack and Janice were once involved was even harder to believe. Looking at the two of them now, Zack looked as if he could be her son.

It was only about five minutes before Zack walked out of the room. "She would like to speak with you, Michael," Zack said, holding the door open for me. I walked into the room. Janice was patting the end of the hospital bed, motioning for me to sit there.

"I know you have many questions," she said to me.

"Yes," I answered. "Far more questions than answers, I'm afraid."

"You'll have your answers soon enough."

"Zack hasn't aged since you knew him all those years ago, has he?"

"No, Michael, he hasn't aged a day. I realized today that I never really knew him. I knew only what he wanted me to know. I don't know exactly what he's planning to do, I only know that whatever it is, you a very big part of it. Do you know what he is?"

"No, I have no idea. I think that's one of the questions I need an answer to."

"I must ask you a favor, Michael."

Janice did not want me to use her last name or the names of her husband and children when I wrote this story. I told her I wouldn't. I said my goodbyes and walked toward the door. "You have some purpose in all this, Michael. I can't tell you what it is, but I do know there's a reason you're here." I looked back at her, half-smiled, and nodded my head.

Janice told me twice that I was part of what Zack had planned. Maybe she was right, though all I kept thinking to myself was that I had more and more unanswered questions. As we left the hospital, I bought a newspaper. I had to know what had been written about Zack's cure for AIDS.

We made our way back to the car. I assumed we would be heading back to the airport, but Zack had other plans. "So, where to now?" I asked him as we pulled out of the parking garage.

"Do you remember what I told them at the CDC, Michael?"

"Yes, Zack, I remember."

"Well, that's where we're headed, though this time we are going to drive there."

I was not thrilled at the prospect of driving from San Francisco to Atlanta, but I didn't exactly have a choice. I decided to look on the bright side and thought maybe Zack would start to talk. I had turned off the sound on my phone and had not checked for messages since we left Atlanta. Now I saw I had one voice-mail message. It was from my researchers and as I suspected there was no Breeze family in the Philadelphia area. In fact, there was no record of a Zackary Breeze anywhere—no driver's license, no social security, no records, period. I wasn't surprised. I'd come to suspect that Zack hadn't told me anything truthful about who he was. I'd soon find out that I could never even have imagined what the truth was.

Grabbing the newspaper, I read the article, and though it did state that all of the children who had been given the injection were in complete remission, it did not mention anything about the vaccine being made available to everyone who had AIDS. In fact, the CDC declined to comment about the story even though they had been given the credit for the cure in Dr. Price's statement to the press. I remembered what Zack had said to the head of the CDC, and I had a feeling I would not want to be her when we got back to Atlanta.

I looked over at him sitting next to me. "Yes, Michael, I know what the article says," he asserted. I guess that meant the conversation about it was over for now.

We drove south through California. Zack seemed to be avoiding the main highways and taking the so-called scenic route. The first day of our trip was uneventful. We stopped only for gas, food, and then a small motel to spend the night.

We did not talk much that first day. I spent most of my time going over all the notes I had made, and listening to the tape recordings with my earpiece. I had come to realize that everything Zack did had a purpose. I'm sure I would soon find out what the purpose was for us to be driving across the country.

We'd had a nice breakfast and were back on the road. We left California behind and were now driving in Arizona. Judging by the signs I was reading, it looked like we were headed toward Phoenix. "Well, Michael, we are almost at our first stop."

"Where would that be, Zack?"

"The Phoenix International Raceway."

"Zack, why are we going to a racetrack? Are we going to watch a race?" I was not exactly a big fan of auto racing, so I was really hoping the answer was no.

"Not exactly," Zack answered. "We are going to have a little bit of fun."

We pulled into the track and headed toward the VIP area. There were about twenty vehicles parked there—everything from limos to a very large truck that appeared to be a car transporter, though not like any transport truck I had ever seen. Zack parked and we walked through the open gates into the raceway.

There was a group of men standing on the track. One waved and started walking toward us. When he got closer, I realized who he was—James Galway, one of the wealthiest and most influential men in the world. The same James Galway who never did interviews, and was once heard saying that newspapers were good for only two things—training puppies and starting fires. I was not sure I was going to be that welcomed at this gathering.

"Zack, it's good to see you. You're right on time." James Galway said, vigorously shaking Zack's hand.

"Is everything ready?" Zack asked. "Yes, we got the car as you requested from Algar Ferrari, and it was delivered about a month ago. I had this crew do everything you asked, Zack. I even had two former Ferrari F1 team members brought over from Italy. I do have to ask you, how do you expect to drive the car after what you had them do to it?"

"No need to worry, James, I'll manage just fine. James, this is Michael Ryan. He's a writer so don't hate him. What he's here to write has nothing to do with you."

I did not exactly get that warm, fuzzy feeling from the look James gave me. He did reach out his hand, which I shook. "Nice to meet you, Mr. Galway," I said.

"We have not met, since I am not really here, do you understand me?" I did understand him, but thought, *sorry James, you just happen to be a part of this, so fuck you, you're in it.*

We all walked out to the track just as they were pushing a beautiful silver car onto it from the side lane of the track. I assumed it was the pit crew's area. "What kind of car is this, Zack?" I asked.

"This, Michael, is the new Ferrari 458 *Italia*." It looked like a space-ship on wheels to me. Two of the men pushing the car were talking back and forth to each other in Italian. I did not understand what they were saying, but from their tone, it didn't sound like they were happy about being here. Zack spoke something to them in Italian and they both stopped talking.

"What is their problem?" I asked Zack.

"They are upset because I had the car modified. They believe I'm messing with perfection, and in their minds, what the factory builds should not be changed."

Zack walked over to the car to look it over. I turned to one of the men standing near me and asked him, "what did he change on the car that has those guys so upset?"

"The car came equipped with a 7-speed, dual-clutch transmission. It uses paddles mounted on the steering column to change gears." I think by the look on my face he knew I had no idea what he was talking about. "Okay, try this. You drive an automatic car, right?"

"Yes," I answered.

"Let's say we removed the transmission and the gear select lever from your car. How would you drive it?"

"I guess you couldn't," I said.

"Okay. Well, your pal over there had us remove the transmission and the paddles from the steering column. That's why they had to push the car out on to the track, though I have no idea how the hell he is going to drive it the way it is now. Oh, and I'm Pete, the telemetry guy, that's if the car needs telemetry."

"What does a telemetry guy do?" I asked.

"I monitor the car's speed and keep the driver aware of any problems on the track."

I started to walk over toward Zack and the car. I wanted to ask him how he was going to drive the car the way it was. Before I could ask him, Zack was at the rear of the car. He spread out his arms and I guess the best way to describe it would be that he gave the car a hug. All of a sudden, the car began to change. The rear of the car got wider and it became a few inches longer. The center console of the car now had a silver gearshift knob on it.

"Holy shit!" I heard Pete say as he walked up behind me. "Who the fuck is this guy?"

James Galway walked past us and over to Zack. "Here are the keys, Zack. We will be up in the booth. Let us know when you're ready to go."

"Thanks, James, but you can hold on to the keys. I won't need them." One of the other men handed Zack a helmet and he put it on before he got into the car.

"Let's go, guys," James said. I followed him and Pete up to the booth. When we got there, we encountered a young couple with two infants. Damn, I thought to myself. Now it makes sense. She was the mother and these were the twins that Zack had saved in Ohio. I guess James Galway must have sensed I had made the connection.

"Yes, she is my daughter and those are my grandchildren," James told me. "And if it weren't for that man down there, none of them would be alive right now. So if doing this for him makes him happy, well that is a miniscule price to pay in return for what he did for my family." I just nodded my head in agreement.

Pete sat down in front of a large monitor and put on a set of headphones that allowed him to talk with Zack from inside the car. He handed me a set of the same headphones, and James was now wearing one as well. "Ready when you are," Pete told Zack. "Just keep in mind you have never driven this track before, so take it slow at first. And you need to give the tires time to heat up."

"Whatever you say," Zack replied.

The car started up. I could hear the engine roar even from this distance. Zack took off. It didn't look to me like he was taking it slowly at all.

"Remember, guy, I told you to take it slow at first. This is *not* slow."

I don't think Zack was planning on listening to what Pete had to say. It looked like he was going faster and faster. "Pete what's his speed?" James asked.

"This can't be right. It says he is doing 240," Pete replied.

"Wow, 240 miles an hour?" I asked.

"Yes! Shit, he just hit 270. This is not fucking possible. That car cannot go that fast and those tires should shred to pieces at this speed."

"Did you happen to load the system with the music that I requested?" Zack asked.

"Yes, Zack, and the sound engineers redid the system inside the car as well," James offered.

"Perfect. It's time to rock and roll. We'll see what this baby can really do."

Suddenly, I heard the beginning guitar notes of a song that brought me back more than thirty years. It was "Mr. Breeze," by Lynyrd Skynyrd. When I heard the lines of the song, "call me the breeze," it hit me—this is where Zack got his name.

"How is he doing out there?" I asked Pete.

"Well, since neither of you two seemed surprised that this guy is out on that track breaking the fucking laws of physics, I'm sure you won't be that shocked to hear that he just hit 310 miles an hour." Pete ripped the headset off and dropped it on the console in front of him. He turned around and he noticed that the cameras were not on. "What the fuck" he said, standing up and walking over to them. "I swear I turned these things on. Did someone turn the cameras off?" Pete asked us.

"I'm sorry, Pete, but I have a feeling they aren't going to work," James told him.

"Well, that is just wonderful. Do you know how many records were set here today?"

"Pete, I suggest you keep everything you saw today to yourself. After all, without proof, I don't think anyone will believe you."

"Well, you're right about that. I'm right here watching this and I'm still not sure I believe," Pete laughed. I guess he had come to the realization that like the rest of us, he should just sit back and enjoy the show.

I made my way back down to the track and walked over to the pit crew, all of whom seemed to be transfixed on the car as it flew by. I didn't know it at the time, but the track was only a mile long. Zack would fly by in the car every few seconds. Not being a racing aficionado, I was unappreciative of just how quickly each lap was completed.

Zack finally had had enough and he pulled the car into the pit area. When he got out of the car, the two mechanics from Italy both walked toward him, said something in Italian, and bowed. James, his daughter, her husband, and the infant twins soon joined us down on the track.

"Did you enjoy yourself?" James asked.

"Yes, that was a lot of fun. It's one of the few things I have never had the chance to do until now. Thank you," Zack told him.

Pete walked over and shook Zack's hand. He told Zack if he ever wanted to race, he would be glad to be part of his crew.

"I think it's time for Michael and me to leave. I want to thank all of you for being here." Zack walked over to each person and shook hands, and then he thanked them once again. When he got to James's daughter, she had tears in her eyes and a big smile on her face. She wrapped her arms around Zack.

"I don't know what you are, or how you did what you did, but I promise you, I will never forget you." Zack did not reply. After she released her embrace, he crouched down to see the twins in their dual stroller. He reached out and took one of each of their hands. The infants both seemed to be staring into his eyes. It was almost as if they knew who he was. After about a minute, they both smiled and started to giggle—if that is even possible for a child only a few months old. Zack stood up and shook their father's hand, and then turned back toward me.

"Let's go, Michael," was all he said as he walked past me and headed out toward the parking lot. I raised my hand and said, "nice meeting all of you," and turned to follow Zack. Within a few minutes, we were back on the road. "Okay, Michael, so what is it that you are just dying to ask me?"

I looked over at Zack, not sure if I should let on that I realized he had lied to me about who he was. What the hell, I decided.

"So, Zack, now I know where you got your name from."

Zack laughed. "Good job, Michael. I guess you checked out my story and found out that Zackary Breeze does not exist."

"Well, Zack, I'm a writer, and I do have to check the facts before I print them."

"I expected as much. In fact, I would have been very disappointed in you had you not. You just need to be patient a bit longer, Michael, and then everything will be explained to you. Can you do that?"

"Yes, I can wait." It wasn't as if I had much of a choice. After driving through Arizona, we spent the night in a motel a few miles into New Mexico.

That evening, I grabbed all my notes and recordings and tried to come to some conclusion about Zack based on what I already knew. Even his diet seemed to make no sense when I thought about it. He loved to eat greasy cheeseburgers and onion rings, but he looked like he did not have an ounce of fat on his body. I never saw him do any type of exercise, and any normal person who ate like he did would look like a minivan. The more I tried to make sense of any of this, the less sense it made. There did not seem to be a single sane or logical explanation for anything I had witnessed. I decided I was not going to find any answers this way, so I went to bed.

The next morning, after stopping at the diner next to the motel for breakfast, we were back on the road. I had toast and coffee. Zack ate a stack of pancakes, three eggs, ham, and a plate of hash browns. I was never much of an eater in the morning and watching Zack eat that much food turned my stomach just a little.

We drove through New Mexico, and then into Texas. I was not paying much attention to where we were, but somewhere near the Texas panhandle, Zack slowed the car down.

"What's the matter?" I asked him. Zack didn't answer me. He just turned right and headed down one of the many roads that intersected the highway we had been traveling on. I had no idea where we were or, for that matter, where we were headed, but Zack had his foot pressed on the car accelerator, so we were going there in hurry. I saw a building coming up on my right side, and as we got closer, I could see it was some sort of restaurant. There was a parking lot off to the side. Zack slammed on the brakes and pulled in. He stopped the car, put it into park, and was out in a flash. He left the car running and the driver-door open.

I got out of the car, and what I saw disgusted me. There was a man beating this undernourished dog that was chained to the tow hook of a pickup truck. Zack grabbed the man by the shirt and threw him so hard, he went right through the wall of the restaurant that was only about three feet from the where he was standing. Zack unhooked the chain from the dog, grabbed the side of the pick-up truck bed, and threw the truck. It smashed into pieces where it landed about a thousand feet away. The dog was trying to get to its feet, but was so badly injured it was unable to stand up.

"Stay here, Michael," I was told in a voice that made me realize it was not a request.

Zack turned and headed toward the restaurant. The dog started to whimper and then let out a faint bark. Zack stopped and turned around looking at the dog. It was as if the dog and he were somehow communicating.

Zack walked back over to the dog and put his hands on the animal. The dog's injuries were instantly healed and it began to grow larger in size. It was in such bad shape when we arrived, I couldn't even tell that it was a German Shepherd, but I certainly could now. The dog had grown to look more like a small pony than a dog, and he was definitely a male pony.

The dog looked over at me and I started to back away. Hey, I've never been scared of dogs, but I had never come across one that was six feet tall before. I heard a police siren, and looked over toward the restaurant. I guess the people inside the building had called the local authorities. I suppose I would have done the same thing if a man came crashing through my wall. Zack waited for the officer to get out of his vehicle before it was suddenly crushed like a pancake. The noise of the car being crushed prompted the officer to pull out his weapon and quickly turn around. He then just fell forward and landed on his crushed vehicle, unconscious and certainly no threat to us. I looked back over at Zack and there was the dog, still looking at me like he was checking out his next meal.

"There is nothing to worry about, Michael, Rover is not going to hurt you."

"Rover, his name is Rover. I'm sorry, did I miss something? I don't recall the dog introducing himself. Why am I even asking this? But you can communicate with him, can't you?"

"Yes, Michael, I can, and he can understand every word you are saying as well."

"Okay, that's it. I have fucking had it," I said, raising my arms up in the air. "I've watched you cure a deadly disease in two hours and heal fatal injuries with a wave of your hand. You've thrown people and trucks around like they are nothing. I've seen you touch a car and it changes shape and goes over 300 miles an hour. You stare at people and get them to do what you want without speaking a word. Fucking guards opened locked doors for us! Your name comes from a rock-and-roll song from the seventies, which of course is not your real name, you just made it up. And now, on our way back to Atlanta to cure more diseases, you crush a car and you make a dog grow six feet tall. And wait, best of all—the dog understands English, and he can communicate with you! Well, Zack, I'm not going anywhere until you tell me who and what the hell you are."

"Are you done?" Zack asked me. I looked over at him and the dog. Zack had a big smile on his face and I swear the dog was smiling at me as well. I guess I must have looked a bit like a toddler throwing a tantrum, but at least I had managed to get my point across.

"Yes, I'm done."

"Okay, Michael, go get your tape recorder. You're not going to want to miss any of this." I grabbed my recorder and turned it on. "I am what you might call an evolutionary hiccup. I came from a time long before humans even knew what time was."

"How long have you been alive?" I asked.

"I'm not exactly sure, but it has been tens of thousands of years. I aged to a certain point, and then I stopped. My body can regenerate, so it's likely I will live as long as this planet survives."

"What did you mean about the hiccup?"

"Well, if humans were to survive another twenty million years, you might just evolve enough to understand as much as I do."

I was more than just a little taken aback. After all, I had come up with a lot of scenarios in my mind about who Zack was, but none of them came even close to this. I could feel my heart beating faster in my chest. I was standing here with a man who could answer all of the questions we have about our past.

"Okay, Zack, so you're telling me you have been alive for as long as human beings have existed?"

"Well, actually, Michael, longer than that. I watched humans evolve. I was here to watch them go from not being able to walk upright and eating their own feces, to evolving into what you are today. When humans were ready, I taught them how to make clothing, how to make fire, even how to draw. The ancient cave drawings your archeologists found are an example.

"I was the first teacher, so to speak."

"Zack, how are you able to do all the things you do?"

I'm glad Zack told me to turn the recorder on. I was in kind of a state of shock and would have never remembered all of this.

"I have the ability to control all things—anything, whether it be living, or not—and to alter matter in any way I desire."

"I'm not a scientist, Zack. What does that mean?"

Zack smiled. I guess even his simple explanation was too complex for someone with my knowledge. "What it means, Michael, is I can control everything on this planet and change it in any way I like."

"I'm trying to understand. You've been among us for all this time, so why make yourself known to us now?"

"You will find that out soon enough, Michael. You wanted to know who and what I am. Well, now you know. That will have to do for now."

I just stood there, still not completely sure about what I had just heard, and I think Zack must have known that.

"I guess you're now convinced that what I told you is the truth."

"Well, Zack, let's be real here. I was not exactly expecting you to be the first human being on the planet. I think I would have felt better if you had told me you were an alien."

Zack laughed, thought for a moment, and spoke. "Look over there, Michael, what do you see?" I looked over in the direction Zack was pointing his finger.

"I see nothing but arid land." I looked back again at Zack.

"Now look," Zack said. I turned my head. There was now a forest where there was nothing a few seconds ago. I began to slowly back up. I had no idea at the time I was even moving, and only hitting the side of Zack's car snapped me out of my trance.

"Oh my God." The words just came out of my mouth on their own. I turned toward Zack. "Okay, I believe. I still don't understand what exactly I'm doing here. What do you want from me?" I asked.

"I told you, Michael, you will find all the answers you're looking for when the time is right, but that time is not now."

"Sorry, Zack, but remember, I'm a writer. How can you expect me to accept that's all for now after what you just told me? If you want me to stay, you're going to have to give me more, *and* your real name."

"Alright, I'll give you more. My name—I have been called many things over the years. I have no given name, so I always made them up as I went along. Some of my names will be familiar to you."

I made the gesture for Zack to continue.

"Alright, Michael, I hope you're ready for this. I have been known as Zeus, Oden, Amun, Moses, and even Jesus. I am known by many names in every culture and religion on earth." As he spoke, his appearance changed. He was showing me the different people he had been over the centuries. I could see where the images of God had come from and the people he had been. "Your people have built statues to honor me. And over the years, they've taken my words and spun them into fairy tales."

"Back up a second, Zack. Are you telling me you were Jesus, the died-on-the-cross-rose–then-came-back-to-life Jesus?"

"Yes, Michael, though I never claimed to be many of the things that ended up being told about me. I have to admit, I never thought about the consequences of the rise-up-from-the-dead thing. Like I said, humans were really not all that bright even then."

"So I guess the whole Christianity thing was an accident?"

"For the most part, yes, though I was quite happy at first with the way it turned out."

I wanted to press him more about what he meant by that statement, but my mind was all over the place. I had once done a story about Egypt, and I suddenly remembered Amun was an Egyptian god. "The pyramids—that was you, you taught them how to build them, didn't you?"

"Yes, Michael, and I if you think about your history, there are many unexplained things. Some of you have theorized that aliens visited this planet."

"I guess there were no aliens," I interjected.

"No, Michael, there were not. In fact, many of the stories that people believe about me did not happen. You see, early mankind had a remarkable talent of justifying every act of nature with a story. There was no flood, and there certainly was no Ark. There *was* a tidal wave that flooded pretty far inland, and homes and livestock did float away."

"I guess Moses, or should I say *you*, never went up the mountain to get the Ten Commandments either, huh?"

"You already know the answer to that, Michael. I don't know where they got the whole commandments thing, but I thought if I gave mankind some guidelines to follow, perhaps people would choose to live according to them. There were no rules of any kind back then, nothing to determine the way people treated each other. I tried to provide those rules, and for certain periods of time and for certain groups, it did seem to work."

"So you gave us religion."

"No, Michael, I gave you my ideas. You gave yourselves religion. If I had given you religion, don't you think I would have given you only one? You made up stories of creation and gods that never existed to serve the purposes of certain groups."

"What do you mean, Zack?"

"Your so-called religions, whether now or in your past, were all created for control. The gods and God were used to keep people in line. Power and wealth belonged to those who were able to communicate with—or interpret the words of—whatever God or gods were being worshipped at the time. All of your religious writings and stories come from something I told your people thousands of years ago. Those stories were retold many times, and over the years they changed to fit the needs of the times."

It suddenly hit me—I was talking to God. "So they thought you were God?" It was not easy for me to ask that question.

"Yes, and not because I ever claimed to be. At first, there was never any mention of gods. I was, as I told you, a teacher. I taught the early humans how to make tools, though I did have to take them away a few times."

"What do you mean by take them away," I asked.

"Well, contrary to what you might have been taught in school, early man was neither that bright, nor that violent. Without my help humans probably would never have made it past the first few generations. It was only after I showed them how to make tools for building and weapons for hunting for food that they became violent. So I took the tools away and after a few hundred years I'd try again, though the results were always the same. I realized that it was best that I let you develop on your own."

"You have been watching us for all these thousands of years?" I asked.

"I have been watching you, Michael, for over 250,000 years."

I heard the words coming from Zack's mouth and I felt a chill run through my body. I was sitting here with the most remarkable person who has ever walked on our planet, and I had so many questions. I didn't know what to ask first. I decided to go for the big one.

"Is there a God, Zack?" Zack laughed.

"I thought you'd get to that sooner or later. I don't know the answer to that question, Michael. Perhaps God put me here to make sure humans survived. I will save you the trouble of asking this question. Yes, I did let some terrible things happen, and I did nothing to stop them from happening."

"Why, Zack? Why would let all those innocent people die?"

"A long time ago, Michael, I had to make a choice. I had to choose between being your savior or your teacher. I decided that I did not want to be your savior. As I look back on that decision, I have come to think that although it was the right decision at the time, it may not have been the right choice as time progressed."

"Do you feel remorse about not stopping those things from happening, Zack? You *can* feel like the rest of us, right?"

Zack shook his head. I could tell he was becoming annoyed by my questions. "I told you, early man was really not that bright, and someone like me whose abilities they were unable to comprehend, well, that must have meant I was—am—a God. I realized that the only way you were ever going to develop past a certain point was for me to disappear from you. I'm sure your scholars have found similarities in different cultures that they cannot explain, similar architecture in places too far apart geographically to have been influential on each other. I have always been here and at times I would lend a hand, sometimes with your knowledge, and sometimes in other ways."

"Are you trying to lend a hand now? Is that one of the reasons I'm here, Zack? I mean, after all, you've lived among us all of these years and never revealed yourself, and now you want me to tell your story?"

Zack laughed. "As I told you, Michael, you will find out why you are here when the time is right. Do not presume to think you know my reasons or my goals. I can guarantee you that whatever you might think, you will be wrong."

"I wasn't trying to do that, Zack, I was just trying to understand," I said, coming to my own defense.

Zack smiled. "I am not angry with you, Michael, but do yourself a favor and be patient. You have been with me a very short time, and you are already jumping to conclusions." I laughed to myself. Of course, he was right. I was trying to insert own answers because Zack had not yet given me the ones I was looking for.

"Are you still with me?" I know Zack knew that I was not about to leave. This had just gone from a great story to the most amazing story of all time—and I had an exclusive.

"I go where you go," I told him.

"Good to hear. Now we need to get going."

Zack walked over to the car and just like he had done with the Ferrari at the racetrack, he altered the vehicle's size to fit our new traveling companion, Rover. While Zack was doing that, I walked over to the dog. "He does understand what I'm saying, right, Zack?"

"Yes, Michael, as I told you, he understands everything you say."

"Rover." I could not believe I was about to start a conversation with a dog. "My name is Michael. Do you know why I'm here?"

Rover nodded his head *yes*. Now that was a little freaky, and I held back the urge to laugh. "Well, I hope that the two of us can become friends." Rover sat down and lifted one of his paws. He wanted to shake my hand. I reached out and took his paw. It was huge, and I could feel the weight of his leg as I shook his paw.

"See, Michael, now you two are friends," Zack said, a smile on his face. I looked over at Rover. He was shrinking. I was just a bit taken aback by that.

"What was that all about?" I asked Zack.

"Rover is just a bit too big to be riding in a car, so he is using his ability to change size when it suits him." I didn't say a word, realizing that from this point on I could not be surprised by anything I saw. I was just going to keep taking notes and making recordings. Like Zack had said, I would find all of the answers I was looking for at some point, so I was going to do my best to be patient until then.

Zack opened the rear hatch of the newly-redesigned SUV, and Rover jumped up inside. There was no longer a back seat in the vehicle, and outside of a small storage area for our bags, the entire rear area was now for Rover. Zack closed the hatch and got in the driver's seat. I walked over to the driver-side window and pointed toward the restaurant. "Are you going to leave these people like this?" I asked.

"Why, Michael? Do you think I should kill them?" Zack answered.

"That's not what I meant, and you know it, Zack."

They will all live, but that piece of garbage who abused Rover will never raise his hand to hurt another animal, or anything else for that matter, ever again. Now please, Michael, get in the car."

I got in and we were back on the road. Before I knew it, we were in Oklahoma. I am sure you're wondering how could I be so calm about all of this. I wish I could give you an answer, but to this day, I have no idea why.

We were driving for less than an hour when Rover suddenly stood up and put his head between the two front seats. "Rover is hungry, Michael. I think we should stop and grab some food." We were driving east on I-40 heading toward Oklahoma City.

"Zack, we should be in Oklahoma City pretty soon. I'm sure there will plenty of places to eat around there."

As always, Zack seemed to know exactly where he was going. Within a few minutes, we were in the parking lot of a Red Robin. The rear hatch of the SUV opened and Rover jumped out of the car. I was pretty sure they were not going to let a dog go in and eat with us, but the hostess walked us over to a large table and seated us. She handed us our menus, smiled at Rover, and told us what a nice dog he was as she walked away.

"So, Rover, what are you in the mood for?" Zack asked as he showed Rover the pictures of the food in the menu. I just laughed to myself. Our waitress came over, introduced herself as Lori, and asked if we would like a beverage. "Well, Lori, I think we are ready to order," Zack said, giving me a look. I nodded that I was ready.

"Okay, what will you gentlemen be having?"

"Well, first, for our friend Rover, I need you to bring two empty salad bowls, two large waters, and a Natural Burger with five extra patties." Lori suddenly had this empty stare on her face, and she looked down at Rover. It looked like she was about to say something, then Zack spoke again. "Did you get that, Lori?"

"Yes, I got it, and how about you two?"

"I'll have the Royal Red with a double patty and the onion rings, and a glass of water."

Lori looked over at me next. "I'll have an iced tea and the grilled chicken salad with Italian dressing." She thanked us and went to put our order in.

It took about ten minutes for our food to arrive, and the whole time not a single person seemed to notice that there was a rather large dog sitting in the restaurant. I am sure that Zack was somehow responsible for that, but at the moment I found it somewhat amusing.

Just as our food arrived, I saw a young boy in a wheelchair coming into the restaurant. The staff seemed to know the boy and they moved things around to accommodate him. Rover, who had finished eating in less than a minute, also noticed the boy, and he watched every move the child made. Rover was now sitting with his back to us, but he turned his gaze away from the boy to look at Zack. I could tell by the look on Zack's face that he and Rover were communicating. Rover seemed to smile as he turned his attention back to the boy and then started to walk toward him. I stopped eating and watched Rover as he approached the boy. Once again, it amazed me that no one was bothered by this rather large dog as it walked through the restaurant. Even the child's parents weren't worried as Rover came close to the boy. The boy reached out his hand to pet Rover when he got closer.

"It's okay, Michael," Zack said. I did not bother to answer him, but I did get up and walk over to introduce myself to Rover's new friends. The boy's name was Robert. He had been hit by a drunk driver two years ago while riding his bike and was crippled for life. Rover was licking Robert's face and the boy was laughing and smiling, enjoying every minute of it. There was something engaging about the boy. He seemed to be full of life and energy, and even though he was no longer able to walk, he seemed happy and well-adjusted. I somehow felt small being around him. I knew I would never be able to handle what had happened to him quite as well.

I looked over to our table and saw Zack getting up from his chair. He walked over to me.

"I heard everything, Michael," he said as he passed me and walked over to Robert. "Hi, Robert, my name is Zack."

"Hi, Zack, is this your dog? What's his name?"

"His name is Rover, Robert, and he's my friend."

Zack looked over at Robert's parents, stood up, and reached out his hand to Robert's father. "Zack Breeze," he said as took hold of Robert's father's hand.

"Frank Jordan, and this is my wife, Karen."

"Michael Ryan." I shook hands with both of them.

"I heard what happened to your son and, if you don't mind, I'd like to help," Zack told them.

"Thank you, but the doctors have told us they've done all they can," Frank told Zack. Karen put her hand on her husband's arm and she leaned forward in her chair, looking at Zack, then at Rover, and then at Frank.

"You're not a doctor, are you?" she asked Zack.

"No," Zack replied. "I am someone who can help. All you have to say is *yes*."

Karen looked at Frank and she grabbed his hand. I could see tears welling up in her eyes. "Frank, I don't know how I know this, but I do. Please. He can help Robert."

Frank looked over at his son and then at Karen, and then back over at Zack. "Mister, if you can help my son, then please do."

109

Zack nodded and got down on his knees in front of Robert. "Okay, Robert, let's see what your big problem is."

As Zack spoke, two images appeared in the air just like what had happened at the CDC. One image was a human body in skeleton form, and the second image was the rest of the inner workings of the human body.

I heard the sounds of silverware dropping on plates, and I heard gasps and oh-my-Gods from the people sitting around us. Frank and Karen were just staring at the images of their son's body, mouths wide open, completely speechless.

"So, Robert, do you feel like walking today?" Zack asked.

"Sure," Robert said. Zack looked back at me as he put his hand on the boy's chest. Zack smiled at me and his appearance suddenly changed. He now looked just like the images I'd had seen of what God was supposed to look like—long white hair and a long white beard, and he was wearing a white tunic. I did not know at the time, but I was the only one who could see him like that. The appearance change only lasted the few seconds that Zack was touching the boy.

"Alright, Robert, let's see you move your legs," Zack told him.

The boy seemed tentative for a moment. He looked over at his mother and father, and then at Zack. Rover walked over to the boy and took his arm in his mouth and began to pull him out of the wheelchair. Robert looked scared for a second, but a moment later he was standing up. He just stood there, not seeming to know what to do next.

"Come on, Robert, take a step. You can walk now," Zack told him. "Go walk over to your Mom and Dad."

Robert took one step and then another. Once he realized he was able to use his legs, he ran around the table twice before his dad grabbed him, picked him up, and hugged him. The people in the Red Robin were now cheering and clapping. Karen Jordan had tears running down her face. She walked over to her husband who was still holding Robert and hugged them both, and then she looked over at Zack.

"What can we say to you?" Karen asked.

Zach replied, "you don't need to say anything. What I see right now is more than enough for me."

Zack looked over at me. I was just sitting there taking in the feelings that were around me. I'm not really sure how to describe it. As I would come to find out, there was a purpose for these feelings, as there was a purpose in everything that Zack did or caused to happen.

Frank put Robert down and he walked over to Zack and Rover. Robert gave Rover a hug around the neck, and then reached out his arm to offer Zack a handshake. "I want to thank you, sir, for helping me," Robert said to Zack, sounding quite grown up.

"Like I told your mom and dad, Robert, you don't need to thank me. And my name is Zack."

"Okay, Zack, can I ask you to do something else?"

"What would that be, Robert?"

"I was in the OU Children's Hospital for a long time after my accident, and there are a lot of kids there who are sick, or hurt like I was. Can you go there with me and help them, too?"

Zack smiled and patted Robert on his head. "Yes, if your parents will lead the way, I will go to the hospital with you and help all the children there."

"Can we go help the other kids, please?" Robert asked his parents.

"Of course we can, son," Frank told him. Even though the manager and pretty much everyone in the Red Robin offered to pay our bill, Zack insisted on paying. We were soon on the road following the Jordan family to the OU Children's Hospital.

"Michael," Zack said, "remember this boy and what he did today." I wasn't exactly sure what he meant by that, but I was sure I'd find out at some point.

It took us about twenty minutes to get to the hospital. After we parked, Robert jumped out of his parents' car. He was jumping up and down, and Rover started to play with him.

"Come on, Robert, let's go inside," Frank said to his son after a few minutes.

We all started walking toward the entrance to the hospital. Zack and Rover were in front, Robert and his dad behind them, and I was lagging behind looking for a new tape for my recorder. Rover had suddenly grown to be a small pony again. I found the tape and was now bringing up the rear. Karen slowed her pace so she could walk with me.

"Who *is* he?" She asked me. I was not about to tell her what I knew, so I decided to just dampen her curiosity.

"He's someone who can help. That's all I know."

"You did notice the dog changed his size, right?" Karen asked.

"Yes, he does do that," I replied, looking to close the subject. Fortunately, entering the hospital put a stop our conversation.

"Come on, Zack," Robert said as he grabbed Zack's hand.

We all walked past the front desk. As I expected, no one said a word or, for that matter, even noticed a six-foot-tall dog walking past them. We made our way to the fourth floor. When the elevator doors opened, Robert ran down the hall.

"Come on, Zack, this way!" he yelled as he ran. We followed him to the nurses' station. The three nurses standing at the counter had a look of disbelief on their faces. One of them had picked up the phone. Then we heard, "Dr. Stein, please come to the fourth floor nurses' station," coming over the loudspeakers.

"Zack, come on, I want you to meet my friends so you can help them like you helped me." Robert grabbed Zack's hand, trying in vain to pull him away.

I heard the sound of the elevator reaching our floor and I looked behind me. Robert did as well, and he ran toward the man who had exited the elevator. "Hi, Dr. Stein!" He yelled. "Look at me, I can run and walk and jump again!"

Dr. Stein stopped and just watched Robert, and then he looked toward us. He looked to be in his mid-forties, tall, fit, and dark-haired, and it appeared he had not shaved in a couple of days. He started walking toward us. Robert was running in circles around him.

"Frank, Karen, I'm not sure I know what to say. What I'm seeing is just not possible, but I cannot tell you how happy I am for all of you," Dr. Stein told the Jordans.

Karen stepped forward and kissed the doctor on the cheek. "I know you did everything you could for us," Karen told him. "And everyone here was always so kind and helpful."

Rover stood up and walked toward the doctor. "My God, is that a dog?" Dr. Stein started to step back.

"It's okay, Doctor. Rover won't hurt you. He's my friend," Robert told him.

"Okay, Robert, I'll take your word for that."

I offered my hand to the doctor. "My name is Michael Ryan, and this is Zack. You've already met Rover."

"Nice to meet you both," Dr. Stein replied. I could tell he was much more interested in finding out how it came about that Robert could suddenly walk than in meeting us. "Frank, how did this happen?"

"Ask him, Doc," Frank said, pointing to Zack. "He simply touched Robert's chest, and he started to walk." The doctor's eyes turned to Zack. He was suddenly very interested in knowing more about us.

"Dr. Stein, Zack cured me," Robert said. "I brought him here to help all the other kids."

"Have a look, Robert," Zack said, his finger pointing down the long hallway. I saw children coming out of their rooms, standing in the hallway, some laughing, others touching parts of their bodies like they were something new that they didn't have before.

It would be hard to describe the looks that the nurses and Dr. Stein had on their faces at that moment—something like awe and shock mixed together. Robert saw one of his friends standing in the hallway and he ran up to him.

"That boy has a degenerative bone disease. He could barely move anymore. This is just not possible," Dr. Stein said.

"Anything is possible, Doctor. You're going to find that every child in this hospital is now in a hundred percent perfect health. I suggest you start calling their parents. I'm sure they'll want to take their children home. Besides, there aren't enough of you to babysit all of them," Zack told him. "Robert!" Zack yelled out. "It is time for us to go."

Robert brought the other boy over to Zack. "Zack, this is my friend Joe."

"It is nice to meet you, Joe," Zack said to him.

"Robert says you cured me. Is that true?" Joe asked Zack.

"Yes, Joe, I made you well," Zack answered the boy, patting him on the top of his head. "Now you go enjoy yourself."

I looked around the hospital and it was a crazy, amazing scene. There were children running, playing, and laughing everywhere, and Zack was right——they did not have enough people to watch them all. I waved good-bye to Frank and Karen as we turned and headed for the elevator.

"Please wait," we heard Dr. Stein yell out. "Who are you?"

Zack stuck his head out of the elevator and yelled back at him. "You can call me Mr. Breeze!" I laughed to myself remembering the song. "Yeah, I know, pretty corny," Zack said to me.

When we got down to the lobby, the scene from the fourth floor was repeated. There were children all around the lobby, playing and having fun. Zack just smiled and we made our way out the front doors and back to the car.

"That was a pretty amazing thing you did back there, Zack. I have never witnessed anything that made me feel that way before."

"Well, Michael, I'm glad to hear that. You're starting to learn."

"Learn what?"

Zack laughed at me. "You'll find out in due time," he said. "Michael, Rover, we have a little over 750 miles to go to get to Atlanta. What do you say we drive straight through?"

"That works for me," I told Zack. I looked back at Rover and he nodded his head *yes*.

"Well, then it's unanimous," Zack said. "Let's go."

Rover and I both fell asleep sometime during the drive to Atlanta, and when I woke up, we were about fifteen minutes from the CDC. "I'm hungry," I said, stretching out in the front seat. I guess Rover was too. He stuck his head between the front seats, tongue hanging out of his mouth.

"Alright, let's go get some breakfast," Zack said. We pulled off the road and parked across from a diner. Rover jumped out of the rear of the SUV and went looking for a place to go to the bathroom. When he was done he came back and joined us.

"I envy you, boy," I said to him. "If I did that I'd be on my way to jail right now." Rover looked at me—I swear he was smiling—and shook his head around, and started walking toward the diner. It was pretty crowded, and I headed straight for the bathroom as soon as we got inside. When I got back to Zack and Rover, they were still waiting. A heavyset woman walked up to us. She did not seem happy to see us—or Rover maybe.

"No pets allowed," she said. Zack liked neither her words, nor her tone. "He is not a pet. If anything, you creatures are my pets, so you will get us a table now and feed us. Do you understand me?"

The woman just nodded her head and brought us to a table. She then turned and started to walk back toward the cash register. "Hey!" Zack yelled. "Forget something?"

She turned around, smiled at us, and said, "Enjoy your breakfast and have a wonderful day, all three of you."

I looked over at Zack, shaking my head, half-smiling. "Michael, I need you to contact the Williamses. Have them call the news people and request that they come back to the CDC. Have them tell the CDC that the man who cured AIDS is back, and he is going to cure *all* diseases today."

I reached in my pocket for my phone. I realized I had turned it off when we walked into the hospital in San Francisco and I had never turned it back on. When I did, I saw that I had seven voice-mails. I knew who the voice-mails were from, and as soon as I ordered my breakfast, I headed outside to call Julie.

"Good morning," I said when she answered the phone.

"Where the hell have you been? Last time I talked to you, you were in Atlanta, and then I see you on the news in San Francisco. Where are you now, Michael?" I could tell she was just a bit ticked off at me.

"I'm sorry, Julie, but things happened so fast. I just lost track of time." Well, that was not completely true, but I knew I did not have the time at the moment to tell her the truth. "We're back in Atlanta, and we're going back to the CDC soon."

"For what?" Julie asked.

"Well, his exact words to me were 'to cure all the other diseases.'"

"Michael, there was also a story on the news last night about a children's hospital in Oklahoma. According to the story, each child in that hospital was completely cured of every disease and illness. "Were the two of you there?

"Yes, Julie, we were there, and, yes, Zack cured those children."

"I'm coming down to Atlanta."

"No, Julie, please don't do that. I know you're concerned about me, but that would be a mistake."

"Why, Michael?"

"Because you never know how Zack is going to react to things. I'm asking you to trust me on this one, Julie. I'm still trying to gain his trust and you being here will not help me do that." I did not like lying to Julie, but I knew her. If she knew who Zack really was, she would be relentless in her questions. I really had no idea how he would handle that, but I was pretty sure it would not be well. "Julie, listen, Zack wants all the news people here at the CDC and I think he wants the whole world to know what he's doing this time. I'm sure you will see what happens here today on television soon."

"Alright Michael. You just be careful, and you keep that phone on."

"Yes, Ma'am."

We said our goodbyes and then I called the Williams family. Melody Williams answered the phone when I called. "Good morning, Melody, it's Michael, Zack's friend."

"I know who you are, Michael, and good morning to you. You boys have been busy. I saw the news in San Francisco and in Oklahoma City."

"Yes, that was Zack. Now we are back in Atlanta."

"Well then, why don't you two come on over for some breakfast?

"I'd love to, but we're at a diner right now. Zack is heading back to the CDC, and he would like you and James to get in touch with the media and have them go over there this morning."

"You know, the hospital suspended Dr. Price after he gave that news conference, and no one will acknowledge that Domenique and the rest of the children were cured."

"I figured as much when I didn't see anything in the papers about the cure."

It's terrible, Michael. They're letting people die when they have a cure. We'll do whatever we can to help. Who should we contact?"

"Everyone, Melody, everyone you can think of. Zack would also like you, James, and Domenique to meet us at the CDC."

"You tell Zack, we'll be there."

I made it back to our table just as the waitress was bringing our food. Zack had ordered for everyone. As I've mentioned before, I was never a big eater at breakfast and the three fried eggs, ham, bacon, and stack of pancakes placed down in front of me was quite imposing. Zack had ordered the same thing for himself, and Rover was having a nice-size steak and a plate of scrambled eggs. "Come on, Michael, eat. We have a big day ahead of us."

"I'll do my best. I spoke with Melody Williams. They're going to contact the media and meet us at the CDC later."

"Perfect," Zack replied.

I did my best to eat as much of my very large breakfast as I could. I have to admit it was really, really good, especially the pancakes. We were all finished eating in less than fifteen minutes, and once we paid the bill we were back on the road headed for the CDC. We pulled up right in front. It seemed Zack was not interested in parking legally. Rover jumped from the rear hatch and he was now grown to horse size—this time well over six feet tall.

Zack walked over to me and put his hand on my shoulder. "Today it begins, Michael. Today the world as you have known it changes forever." I did not yet know what Zack meant by what he said, but his words sent a chill through my entire body.

We walked toward the front doors of the CDC. This time the doors and the part of building that surrounded them disappeared. The guards approached us, but when they saw Zack and Rover enter the building, they stopped and just stood there. "I want you to bring every single person in this building here right now," Zack commanded. "Do you understand me?" Use as many people from security as you need to, but do it now." The guards just nodded their heads and walked away. Within a few minutes, the lobby area began to fill up with people.

Dr. Hale saw us and came over to say hello. "Mr. Breeze, please understand my hands were tied. I was not allowed to say anything, or even acknowledge what happened here.

"I understand, Doctor. We are going to change all that today. I promise you. I will need the cooperation of you and your team."

"You'll have it, Mr. Breeze, I can assure you of that."

Rover started to herd the people to one side of the lobby as if he were a sheep dog herding the animals into a pen. I then heard a female voice call out, "what is going on here?" I looked over and saw our old pal, Dr. Walker, head of the CDC. She was walking toward us, waving her hands in the air like she was trying to clear a smell out of a room.

Rover stepped right into her path causing her to stop in her tracks. Though she did not utter a sound, you could see the fear in her eyes. Rover looked over his shoulder at Zack and me. I looked at Zack, and he just smiled at Rover. Rover turned his head back toward Dr. Walker, and almost immediately she was airborne and thrown into one of the walls of the lobby. She was put in the same position that was used to crucify people, though without the nails hammered into her feet and hands.

Rover went back to his task of herding the group, and Zack walked toward Dr. Walker. At the same time, the Williamses were walking into the building. Domenique wanted to run to Zack, but James, seeing what was going on, held her back.

"I warned you what would happen if any more people died from a disease I had given you a cure for." Zack spoke to her, his voice full of

anger. "Do you know how many people have died just in the last week?"
Dr. Walker did not speak. She was white as ghost and obviously terrified.
"I asked you a question, you piece of garbage. Answer me." Zack's voice
became even louder and angrier.

"No, I do not." Her voice was shaking.

"Well, 42,607 men, women, and children have died since I gave you
the cure to distribute around the world. You could have saved those people
if you had done what I told you to do. I know what you're thinking doctor,
and no, I am not going to kill you, though I should. You are going to stay
exactly as you are and you are going to watch what happens here today,
and while you do, you are going to feel the pain and the suffering of every
person who lost someone you could have saved."

Zack turned and walked away from her. When he saw the Williamses, a
smile came to his face. James, Melody and Domenique walked toward him,
though Domenique started to run. When she got to Zack, he picked her up
and hugged her. "How is my little angel doing?" Zack asked her.

"I feel great, Zack. Are you going to cure more people?"

"Yes, that is why we are here today."

"What's that?" Domenique asked, pointing over at Rover.

"That, Domenique, is my friend Rover."

"Why is he so big?"

Zack laughed. "Don't worry, he might be big, but he would never hurt
you. Come with me, I'll introduce you to him."

While Zack walked Domenique over to meet Rover, I walked toward
James and Melody. Melody gave me a hug and I shook James's hand. "We
called everyone we could think of, Michael," Melody told me.

"What is with that dog? That thing is, like, seven feet tall," James said.

"That dog's name is Rover and, by the way, he understands every word you say."

"Was that really necessary?" Melody asked me, pointing toward Dr. Walker.

"Look, I'm just here to tell his story, and I doubt he cares whether I like what I see or not. I do know this much—he intends to make sure that they can't keep the cures a secret after today."

"We called all of the parents who were here that day," Melody said. I think a lot of them will show up as well."

Zack and Domenique walked over to join us. Zack said hello to the Williamses and then looked over to me.

"Everything you asked for has been done, Zack. What's next?" I asked. Rover had walked up behind me and, in a gesture that took me by surprise, rested his head on my left shoulder. I froze for a moment, not sure what to make of his actions.

Zack chuckled when he saw my reaction, and then he handed me an envelope. "The media are getting set up outside, Michael. I want you to read this statement to them once they are ready. You can use the podium right out front."

What podium? I thought to myself. But when I turned to look at the front of the building there was now a podium. "Rover will go with you. He will make sure no one interferes with what we are doing in here."

"Alright, Zack, I'll do what you ask, but you need to do something for me."

"What, Michael, what would you like me to do for you?"

"Let her go," I said, pointing toward Dr. Walker. "I thought we were here to help people, not hurt them," I told Zack. "You think this was just her decision, Zack? Come on, you know better than that."

Zack smiled at me. He seemed happy that I had stood up for Dr. Walker. He walked past me, patting me on the shoulder. He gently let Dr. Walker down from the wall. Zack walked over to her and helped her to her feet. He motioned for the guards to come over and told them to escort her from the building.

"I would like everyone's attention please," Zack yelled out. There was an almost immediate silence and everyone turned their attention to Zack. "Everyone please move to the front of the building." Zack motioned with his hands for them to walk forward. Once we were all standing near the front of the building, Zack turned around to face all of us. "Today, with your help, we are going to cure all diseases known to mankind, and we will do it while the whole world watches."

As he spoke, the entire floor was altered. It was turned into one enormous lab with all the workstations and equipment that would be needed. "Okay, let's get to work," Zack told them. I have no idea how they all knew where to go and what to do, but they did, and they all just went to work. Zack walked over to me and said, "It's your turn now, Michael."

"I'll do the best I can," I answered.

"Remember, say only what is written and answer no questions."

"I think I got that part, Zack." I turned and started to walk toward the podium, Rover walking beside me. Domenique ran over and took my hand. I guess she was coming with me as well.

I got to the podium and looked out in front of me. There were about fifty men and women with cameras and microphones all pointed at me.

Over to the left, I saw a group of children and their families. They were the children Zack had cured the last time we were here. I was used to reporting a story, not being part of it, and I guess even Domenique could tell I was not entirely comfortable standing there.

"You'll be fine," she told me, letting go of my hand. Domenique and her parents went over to join the rest of the group of children and parents.

I took a deep breath and as I looked over to my right, I saw that Rover was in a seated position a few feet away from me. He was at least two feet taller than I was when I was sitting down. Shit, I thought, seeing how fucking big he was now. I opened the envelope Zack gave me and unfolded the paper inside. "Good morning, my name is Michael Ryan, and I would like to read you this statement on behalf of my friend. Please keep in mind there will be no questions taken."

"A short time ago, I came here and found a cure for AIDS, a cure which was used on the children you see before you. I offered that cure to the world for free. That offer was refused, and because of that, thousands have died needlessly. I come here once again, this time, to find cures for every disease that exists. Because you can't seem to be trusted to do what is right, everyone on the planet who is afflicted with a disease will be healed the moment the cure for his disease is developed. You will also be given the cures for all future diseases to use as needed. Who *I* am is not important at this point in time. The man who is reading this statement will be telling my story in a book he is writing. You will find all the answers to your questions in his book. What occurs here today will be seen all over the world, and any attempt to stop that from happening will fail. Also, any attempt to stop what is being done here today will not be tolerated. Anyone who approaches this area with that intent will be dealt with severely. Enjoy the music."

I took a couple of deep breaths after I finished reading, and of course a few idiots raised their hands to ask questions. I shook my head and turned around then headed back into the building. Rover stayed where he was. Zack was waiting when I walked back into the building.

"Good job, Michael," he said to me.

"Zack, what was the 'enjoy the music' thing?"

"Oh that," he answered, and instantly the music of the Grateful Dead began to play. I had been to a few Grateful Dead shows myself earlier in my life and was very familiar with their music. The odd thing was that for a brief period of time that day, the entire group became Deadheads. When "Sugar Magnolia" started playing, I looked around and everyone was moving to the music. What I didn't realize at the time was that the music was being simultaneously broadcast on every TV and computer screen on the planet, and people around the globe were dancing to its beat.

I watched as the researchers worked non-stop inside the CDC. Zack sent me out to announce each disease as soon as its cure was discovered. The first was cancer, all types. Then diabetes, malaria, tuberculosis, arthritis, autism, and many others. It went on for nine hours. Every few minutes I would announce that another disease had been cured. I know many of you saw all of this live on your televisions, but what you did not see that day was Zack giving the doctors and researchers at the CDC the ability and the knowledge to achieve this amazing feat. If you ask any of them today how they did what they did, they will tell you they have no idea and no memory of it.

I *do* remember that day, and I will never forget it. By 10:00 a.m. almost all of Atlanta had shut down. People poured out into the streets and they cheered with the announcement of each disease that had been cured. Like I said earlier, everyone was a Deadhead that day, and everyone, young and old, was dancing to the music. I looked out at a sea of people, all gathered at the CDC, all wanting to be a part of what was happening there.

I must admit it was kind of amusing for me to see people I know—people who probably never even heard of the Grateful Dead or listened to their songs—dance like they were high on the music. I could not help thinking to myself, I wonder what Jerry Garcia would think if he were here to see this? I have to say that for the first time in my life, I had a true feeling of pure goodness all around me. It was a feeling I had never known before and have never felt since.

By the time they were through, Zack had done exactly what he had promised. He had cured every disease known to mankind. When I looked out onto the streets of Atlanta, there was nothing but people as far as the eye could see. The last song that played that day was "Brokedown Palace." I had to smile as the words seemed very fitting for what had occurred.

I walked inside the CDC. Everyone looked exhausted but immensely happy. "I guess you're done here," I said to Zack.

"Just about, Michael. I'll be right out," Zack answered.

I walked back outside and looked over at the huge crowd, wondering how the hell we were going to drive through all these people. All of a sudden, I heard a collective gasp from the crowd and they were all pointing in my direction. I turned to see what was behind me.

It was Zack, but he had changed his appearance to show the world what he showed me for only an instant that day he cured Robert. I guess the combination of what he had done here today and his God-like image was enough to overwhelm most of the massive crowd, as many dropped to their knees.

Zack walked up to me. I looked over at him. "What is this all about Zack?" I asked. "For everyone to think you are God again?" I gestured my arm out toward the crowd. "Look, they're all on their knees for you, Zack."

"It is time for you to know your purpose, Michael. Follow me."

Zack and Rover walked over to the Williamses. They too were on their knees. Zack reached out his hand and touched James's shoulder, and James looked up at him. I could see the look on his face was part fear and part reverence.

"Stand up, James. You too, Melody," Zack told them. They slowly began to stand and as they did, Zack bent to pick up Domenique. He hugged her and kissed her cheek before putting her down next to her parents.

"I want to say goodbye," he told them.

"I don't know what to say to you," James replied.

"You are good people," Zack said, "and you deserve better than what your world has become."

"Will I ever see you again?" Domenique asked him. Zack did not answer her question. He just turned and began to walk away. I waved to them as I turned and followed him. As we approached the crowd, the people moved backward making a path for us to walk through. We never took a step into the crowd, and the next thing I knew, we were on a beach! At first, I was just a bit freaked out. I had no idea where we were or how we had gotten there. Zack had changed his appearance back to the way he looked when I had first met him, and Rover was running up and down the beach.

"Everything is okay, Michael," Zack said in a voice meant to calm me down. "We traveled in the car at first just for your benefit, Michael. Since you now know what I am, I don't think we really need to use the car any longer." *Speak for yourself*, I thought. I still wasn't sure I wasn't just going to throw up from the sudden transition.

I finally managed to stand up straight and take a few steps along the beach. "Why are we here, Zack?" I asked. "Well, Michael, it's time for you to know your purpose. You are here to give mankind one last chance to save itself."

My head slowly stopped spinning and Zack's words began to register. "What does mankind have to save itself from?" I asked.

"Me," he replied.

"I don't understand. What do you mean?"

"You are here, Michael, to write my words, to impart my message to the world one more time. I have watched you humans for tens of thousands of years. At first you were pitiful, and then merely amusing, like so many puppies chasing their tails. Now what I see disgusts me. Mankind has become nothing but a waste of existence. I brought you here to travel with me for a short time, so you can make sure my words are written the way I mean them and that their meaning is clear."

"*You* brought *me* here?"

"Come now, Michael, did you really believe any of this was your idea?" Zack laughed as he spoke to me. "Yes, I chose you. In fact, I have been looking for someone like you for a long time."

"Someone like me?" It suddenly hit me that nothing that I had done from the first time I thought of writing the story that brought me here was ever my idea. It had been Zack all along.

"You are an unbeliever Michael. You believe in nothing. Not God, not religion, not anything."

"Yes, but I'm certainly not the only one like that."

"That is where you are wrong. Yes, there are others, but their non-belief comes from life's experiences. You were born that way. You never believed, even as a child. You believe in nothing, not even the fairy tales your mother used to read you. Even now you are feeling nothing. You do not know what it is like to love, or to be loved. You tell Julie that you love her because that is what you think you should say, not because it is really what you feel. You are fifty-two years old, never married, no real attachments. You see people as a means to the end, and nothing else. You are an empty shell, and you can write, so you were perfect for this task."

Mr. Breeze

No one had ever spoken to me like that before, and certainly no one else knew these things that Zack knew about me. He was right, of course. I was exactly what he described me to be. I had always been a loner, never letting anyone get that close to me. Even Julie had no idea who I really was. She only saw the person I wanted her to see.

"Okay, Zack, so what message am I supposed to convey to the world?"

"The message is this: If mankind cannot learn to live together in peace, and as equals, I will destroy all of you and start over again."

I was not prepared for that answer and my legs began to shake. I became dizzy and I dropped down to the sand. "What gives you the right to do that?" I asked, my head between my knees as I spoke.

"Because I can," he answered.

"But why, why would you?"

"Just look around your world, Michael, what do you see? Have people learned anything over all these years? No, they have only learned to be more hateful, more selfish, and more destructive to each other."

I had seen his power and I knew he was capable of anything, and I did not know what I could say that would make a difference, but I knew I had to say something. "What do you want from us?" was all I could come up with. He found my statement amusing and just laughed at me.

"You ask what I want from you. Perhaps you should ask what you want for yourselves. You have not progressed as a people. If anything, you have regressed. "Even today, you enslave each other. You value money and power over humility and virtue. No, Michael you have gone backward, forgotten what it even means to be human. Rover has more humanity in him than most people, and I am tired of waiting for you to realize how despicable you humans have become."

I stood up and faced him, somehow empowered to fight for our exist-ence. "Zack, please look at all we have accomplished."

"What have you accomplished, Michael? You value the accomplish-ment of celebrities, sports stars, and business people more than those of people who spend their lives helping others. You have no values. You have nothing but greed and hate. I should have never let this go on as long as I have, but I had such high hopes for you."

"What do you expect me to do? You are asking me to try to save man-kind, but I am just one man."

"What I want from you is simple, Michael. I want you to write what you saw and what I have said. That's all you have to do."

"To what end, Zack? Do we get to live on if everyone reads the book I write?"

Zack laughed at me once again. "Okay, Michael, let me make this sim-ple and clear so you can understand my meaning. If the human race, despite what I have done and what they will read, does not begin to change, and if people are still interested only in self-pursuits and self-gain, then I am going to wipe out every human being over the age of one who lives on this planet. I'll start all over and build a new society—a society without money, without classes, and no haves and have-nots. Everyone will be equal."

"No money?" I asked.

"That's right, Michael. Thousands of years ago, I tried to teach you that money was wrong. But you know what happened?" I shook my head no. "Well, let me tell you then. Those who wrote your Bible, as you call it, were greedy. They lusted after money, and power as well. They twisted my words and my teachings, turning things in any way it suited them. They even went so far as to say give God your money, it shows your faith in him. Zack laughed. "I have no need of your money, but those who promoted your religions did, and they became rich and powerful. That is now over forever. You see, Michael, even if I do let mankind survive, people will pay a heavy price for what they have become. A price, I am sure, you can all learn to deal with if it means you get to live on. You might not feel that way once I tell you the price you have to pay."

"What is the price, Zack?"

"First, your weapons. They will all be destroyed. Let's see how good you are at killing each other with sticks and stones. You will live as one people without separation by country, or race, or religion. Now that you all will know the truth, I think it's time you realized that your religions never came from me. Your technology that you seem so proud of will be destroyed. You will learn once again to speak to each other. Your children will play outside in the fresh air, not in front of a box toying with imaginary games of violence. That is only the beginning, Michael. The price will be very high, and I do not have much faith in your success, so I doubt it will even matter."

"There are some good people, Zack, like the Williamses of this world. What about them?"

"You ask me that question, but what you're really asking is what about you, my messenger?"

"Alright, what about me?"

Zack smiled. "You have mistaken this relationship as friendship, Michael. We are not friends. You serve a purpose. That is all you are to me."

"What if I refuse to write this book?"

"Well then, I will just destroy all of you right now. Is that what you want? Because that is the other option."

"No, I'll write the book. I just don't know how it's supposed to change people. How can one book change the way billions of people think?"

131

Once again, Zack laughed at me. "You let me worry about that part, Michael. You just write the book."

It suddenly dawned on me that he did expect it to change things right away. "We have time, don't we, Zack? You *are* giving us a chance to save ourselves."

"Very good, Michael, and yes, I am going to give you time to save yourselves. We are going on a little tour, Michael. I want you to see what I see." The next thing I knew we were transported to somewhere else, somewhere in Africa, judging by the people and the surroundings. "Look around, Michael, these people have nothing. They fight to survive everyday of their lives, and they do not always win that battle. No one cares what happens to them, no one really does anything to help. They fear for their lives and there is no one to protect them. Armed bands of fighters shoot them for sport, Michael. This is the progress you speak of."

Zack had once again changed his image to the likeness we have come to know as God. The people saw him and began to gather around him. "I have brought you food, shelter, and protection," he told the crowd. He pointed in the direction of the huts which had been transformed into small homes, and there were boxes of food everywhere.

"They will come and take this from us!" someone yelled out from the crowd.

"No, they will not. No one with a weapon will ever come near you again. They are now safe, Michael. Anyone with a weapon that comes within one mile of the village will immediately perish."

I guess Zack had decided he had made his point, since the next thing I knew we were in yet another place.

"We are in Jerusalem, Michael, I have lived here many times over the centuries. This should be a city of hope for your people, but it has become a place of hatred instead. Your people claim it to be a holy place. The funny thing about that Michael is I made it such a place, yet that was never my intention."

Zack was still in the guise of the God-like being and it did not take long before we were noticed. I knew just enough about the Middle East to be misguided in conversations with others when the subject came up. I always thought it was far more complicated than anyone looking from the outside could possibly understand, but I was about to find out otherwise.

Zack grabbed an Israeli and an Arab and threw them on the ground in front of him. The two men knew who Zack was after what happened at the CDC just as most of the world did. They were both scared and each assumed a position of deference to Zack.

"Get up, you fools!" Zack barked at them. The men stood up, but both lowered their heads, their chins buried in their chests. "Look at each other," Zack commanded them. They did as they were told. "You hate each other, you want to destroy each other. Do you have a clue why? I asked you a question!" Zack was now screaming at them. I wasn't sure whether they didn't really know or they were just too scared, but neither could answer him.

"I think they might be too scared to answer you, Zack."

"Michael, they cannot answer because they do not know, and what they do know is wrong. What if I told you all this hatred goes back to money owed for a few sheep thousands of years ago?"

"What are you saying? This has nothing to do with religion?"

"Michael, if you took DNA from these idiots, you'd find they are all related, and it has nothing to do with religion. You see, people have become so used to hating, they no longer know how to live without it. What would you do if you didn't have someone to hate?"

I had no answer, no reply, and no defense to that statement. Zack was right: we have become a people who seem to be better at hate than love.

We were once again transported somewhere else, but this time I knew where we were. We were in Ohio. I had done a story on the militia movement about a year ago, and had spent time with the group from this area. They had built a compound-like structure where they practiced their maneuvers, but they also held family gatherings there. There was snow on the ground and some of the men were playing in the snow with their kids.

Zack was back to his mortal-looking form and was watching something else. I turned to see what he was looking at and saw men with guns and white camouflage suits approaching the compound. They were moving slowly and staying very low to the ground. "Zack, you need to stop this. I know these people. This is exactly what they have been waiting for, a reason to fight back."

"I know, Michael."

"Well then, please stop this. These are not bad people. Their beliefs may not be mine, but they haven't hurt anyone."

"Why should I do anything Michael? It's just another day of you people killing each other."

"Zack, there are children there." I pointed to the children playing in the snow. Zack didn't answer me, and somehow I knew he had no intention of doing anything to stop this.

Just a few seconds later, one of the militiamen spotted the federal agents approaching and gunfire broke out. I guess the children must have known to hit the ground, because all of them did, all but one. He was just a toddler, maybe three years old.

I don't know what came over me at that moment. I had never done anything that would be close to heroic in my life, but I ran toward that child and grabbed him and tried to get him to safety. I felt this sharp pain in my leg and fell to the ground, shielding the boy with my body. I had been shot in the thigh and I was unable to move. A federal agent was coming toward me, his gun pointed right at my head. Rover came from nowhere and put himself between me and the agent. The agent pointed his gun at Rover, but it would turn out be the last thing he did that day. Rover was on him in an instant, snapping the rifle in half with his mouth and then head-butting the agent. I watched Rover grow to ten feet tall. He looked out at both groups. There were wounded men on both sides lying on the ground. He first looked at the agents, sending two of them flying through the air, slamming them into trees. He then turned and did the same thing to two members of the militia.

Their weapons suddenly disappeared and all of them raised their hands in surrender. Rover walked back over to the child and me. "Thank you, Rover," I said to him, still shaking. He nodded his head and walked away. Within a few minutes, the place was teeming with official vehicles and ambulances to take care of the injured. I thought for sure Zack would just cure me, but instead he let them load me into one of the ambulances. He and Rover walked over to me before they took me away.

"It is time, Michael. Go write the story." He put an envelope in my pocket. "You put these words at the end of the book, Michael."

"How long, Zack, how long do we have?" Zack didn't answer me and the doors to the ambulance closed. That was the last time I saw him. In fact, no one has seen him or Rover since that day.

That was eight months ago, and I still don't know how long the human race has before its possible demise. Even though I may not be exactly what Zack wants me to be, I do know that I am not the same man I was before I met him. Maybe that's what he expects—if each one of us takes a step in the right direction, maybe someday we'll all get to the place he wants us to be. I hope after you read this you'll decide to take that step. Considering the other option Zack gave us, it may be our only chance.

When I opened the envelope Zack gave me, this is what he had written:

"I realize I may not be the heavenly father you have come to believe existed. That is my fault. I gave you that image when you were young. Though I did raise you and I chose to bestow free will upon you, you have used that gift to learn to hate, to kill, to become bitter and selfish, and to care only for yourselves. You have even learned to hurt your children and to subjugate your fellow man. I tried to teach you the lessons you needed to learn to live in peace and harmony with each other, and you chose to ignore them. So now I give you one last chance to be what I always hoped you could be. Whether or not mankind continues is up to you. Learn well this time, my children. I will not be patient much longer."

www.ingramcontent.com/pod-product-compliance
Lightning Source LLC
Chambersburg PA
CBHW051252170626
46809CB00004B/1605